AFTER THE PARCH

Sheldon Greene

Other novels by Sheldon Greene

Lost and Found

Burnt Umber

Prodigal Sons

Pursuit of Happiness

The Seed Apple

The Lev Effect

Tamar

"After being turned out of his earthly paradise, Candide wandered off without thinking which way he was going." Candide, Voltaire

"Wedged between ocean, mountains, and desert, California Republic shows promise of becoming a wasted place of exile, a prison without restraint, an asylum without treatment, a poor house without alms, an arena of boundless opportunity and limitless despair." A Pocket History of the Dissolution, Hugh Cress, Cosmo Press, 2064.

October 25, 2075

Forest Service
District 39
California Republic

THE FIRST DAY

The road lurches over the hillside, staggers through a few turns and shrinks to one lane next to a rusted green sign so faded that only the town name, "Templeton" and the "Forest Service Center" are legible. Worn away by time, weather, and indifference, the mileage is forgotten. It doesn't matter. Except for the stage buses, strangers seldom travel the road and, even if they do, they can see the District Administrative Center even before coming to the sign. The spear-straight firs that had once covered the gentle slope and obscured the view of Templeton are now just a memory recalled by a cemetery of bleached and rotten stumps. Templeton is as Bran has always known it; green, slope-roofed, homely buildings, baled like recycled newspapers by its sixteen-foot high double barbed-wire fence.

Bran looks at Mavis and eases Morningstar, his roan mare, around the section of the pavement that had collapsed after a long-ago slide. Every pitch and pothole of the road are as familiar to him as the teeth in his mouth. For the last three years, since his fifteenth birthday, he has ridden it once a week to pick up the little mail that the Glade receives. Outlaws of the highest class since the Dissolution of the United States, the Glade community pays no taxes but gets no public services. Since the

General Land Distribution, the community of no more than forty families has lived in a narrow enclave in the forest; gardening, grazing their sheep, apart from the world they reject and fear.

And now in just ten days Bran must bring the Glade into the greater community or they will be thrown off their land. Hidden in the lining of his pack is a fortune, $20,000 Old Dollars. Never having gone further than Templeton, he must travel to the other end of California Republic to a place called Irvine and register a long overdue claim to the land before it is forfeit forever.

"Scared?" asks Mavis as she and her dappled bay mare come up to him. She looks at him, the forget-me-not blue of her narrow eyes bleached by the morning sun.

"No," he replies in a muffled unconvincing way. Recalling something, he says with an undercurrent of amusement, "the Elder gave me a map; so old I'm afraid to open it." He turns to look at Mavis. "Micah looked at the map and said I'd be lucky to get as far as Templeton with it. And he is right. Templeton isn't even on it."

"As long as Los Angeles is, you'll make it," she says, her voice soft and reassuring. Bran isn't so sure. Had the Elder told him to run the fifteen miles to Templeton and back he would have done so with more innate confidence than he felt approaching this journey alone.

"I still can't figure out why they picked me."

"You're the best, that's why. You're strong, you can make snap decisions just like you do on the hyde ball field."

"Abner's smarter, and just about as strong."

"Abner cares too much about himself to have thrown himself under the wheels of a backing truck to save the life of a child, as you did." says Mavis, looking at him with admiration and wonder.

"It was sort of like diving for a hyde ball. I had no time to think about it. I just landed on Phil and rolled with him between the tires. And if you think it is courageous you should have seen how my hands shook afterward."

"Bran, bravery comes straight out of your heart. It's either there or it isn't."

He smiles and feels self-conscious. Praise, even coming from someone who loves him, always embarrassed him. For sixteen years, since Ragnar had found him on the road clutching his dead mother, Bran has been nurtured by the Glade. Raised by Leah, Mavis's mother, as one of her own children, Bran has lived in the same room with Mavis and brawled with her brother, Peter. Taught to be a skilled gardener and a shepherd, Bran knows virtually nothing of the world beyond Templeton. It is a fog to him.

At least they might have sent two of us, Bran thinks. Things could happen and no one would know about it. The pack could be stolen, he could be murdered. The roads are full of robbers, people say. But the Elder thought that one poor young man traveling alone would attract the least attention.

Mavis coughs, the dry residue of a cold. She is wearing the deerskin pants and soft store-bought white cotton shirt that he gave her for her eighteenth birthday. Bran studies her, trying to etch the details in his mind as if for the first time. Her hair, the faded golden shade of a mountain meadow in late summer, gleams softly and falls in an arc over her sun- browned cheek. Her narrow, blue eyes turn toward him, gentle as always, looking like they know his thoughts.

"They could of sent us both," he says, thinking how good she is at smelling danger before it arrives.

She answers with a rueful no, and coughs again, her hand over her mouth.

A chickadee calls, and Bran turns to see it peer into a hole in the bark of a tree. The mine comes to mind, midway up the western flank of the Glade, the grey scar of its tailings running almost to the base of the slope. A frightening place, its reaches dripping and unknown, the cave has always drawn them to it. To keep children from straying into the tunnel, Micah, the head gardener, used to say that the soughing of the wind on the ridge is the cry of the trapped miners and for many years Mavis had believed him. And now the mine posed a real threat. Some company wanted to reopen it and has filed a claim to the entire valley.

"Remember the time I killed the rattler up at the mine and put it under Peter's bed?" he says.

The memory of it reflected in her eyes, she says, "The scar on your forehead sometimes reminds me." Peter had wrestled Bran to the ground and bashed his forehead against a rock. "He was furious."

"It doesn't take much to make him mad." The mine has other memories for them both. Years ago, they had been caught by a sudden spring rain and taken shelter inside the cave mouth. There they had first known each other as mates.

"Don't forget to ride Morningstar or at least let her run by herself. She won't wander too far." He says this in the few minutes before they would part at the stage bus, knowing that it might be for the last time. Somehow, he never has the right words in his mouth.

"Yes," She looks away again and he studies her profile, the upper lip tilted and set ahead of the lower, the little smile fixed in the corner of her mouth. Caleb, his black and white mottled sheep dog, is trotting by his side looking up expectantly. Often as not, he didn't go along on the ride into Templeton, preferring his own amusements around the Glade. This time, perhaps he understands that this trip is special, Bran thinks.

A fast trot takes them to the town gate, watched listlessly by an elderly Forest Service officer in his sun-faded green uniform. He waives Bran in, and they ride between the unadorned square wood houses, drab as poverty, toward the wide square. A thin woman in a brown loose-fitting dress sits on a stoop, knitting, and takes no notice of them. Nearby, two khaki clad legs protrude out from under a faded, banged-up pickup truck, its hood open like a mouth. Why, he wonders, do they bother to keep those wrecks going when a horse would forage for itself, require no impossible-to-obtain parts, and even be a companion to the rider?

Mavis looks around and says, "This is such a sorry place. I hate coming here."

"I'm used to it. After a while you stop seeing the things that bother you."

They ride into the town center and see the wide, two-story wooden Forest Service Administration Building. Two sides of the square have one-story shops that sell necessities and a few luxuries; clothing, hardware, tools, flour, rice and small quantities of tea and coffee for those who can afford them. The Templeton Theater alternated films with live entertainers. Its flat marquee advertises a variety show and a Tarzan film. Bran looks at it with the same curiosity he always felt, as he has never been to a film. The people at the Glade thought that making your own entertainment is healthier than watching someone else's. Maybe he would see one on this trip, if things went smoothly, and he got to Los Angeles in three days as planned. And why shouldn't he; the stage buses run from district to district. He has only to go from one to the other. Bran gazes at the other buildings; the three bars, the two cafes-one with tablecloths, one without-and the Casino, where people played the stock market game or rolled dice.

Opposite the administration building is the stone courthouse and jail and two churches: one with a spire, one without. A few cars, dusty, oxidized and dented, are parked in front of the shops along with some pickup trucks. Farmers are setting up tables or cloths on the ground in the grass-covered square and elderly men, their clothes faded and washed too many times, are lounging in front of any store that provided a bench, or sitting on the public benches in the square, bent over checker boards or cards.

As always, a few homeless children, motley as the ever-present congregation of dogs, are looking around hopefully for their next meal. Bran thinks of Ephus, the boy that he had picked up on the square and brought back to the Glade just six months before. He still refused to sleep on a bed and was only now getting used to shoes. He had formed a strong attachment to Bran, following him everywhere. "See if you can keep Ephus from running off, Mavis." He had wanted to go along on the trip with Bran and when Bran had refused, Ephus had run off into the woods to sulk. He hadn't even been around that morning to say goodbye.

"If he does, he'll just come back when you do." Mavis has a way with young children-one of her jobs is caring for them while their parents are working-but so far Ephus has eluded her.

A gaggle of farmers surrounds the door of the red and blue striped, snub-nosed bus parked in front of the Evergreen Cafe.

The bus driver is still on the roof receiving boxes and bundles and tying them down.

"I guess this is it," says Bran, swinging out of his saddle and dropping the reins on Morningstar's smooth neck. Bran unties his pack and slings it loosely over one broad shoulder.

Mavis also swings down. Holding the reins in her left hand she looks up at him, love mingling with sadness in her level gaze, and says, "I packed some extra things at the last minute. You never know what you'll need. And Mom's food is in the outside pocket where you can get to it." She reaches up, caresses his thick, sable-dark hair and gazes thoughtfully into his gold-flecked green eyes. Her own eyes brighten under tears. She sniffs and forces her lips into a smile of apology as he wraps his arms around her and holds tight.

"How much time to we have?" she asks, looking sidewise at the bus.

"Just enough to say goodbye."

"Then take this for the road," and she reaches around his neck and kisses him softly. "And remember that I love you."

"I'll be back so soon you won't even have time to miss me."

The last of the passengers carrying their smaller bundles have boarded and the driver says, "Better get on if you're coming or you'll have a whole day to kiss that pretty girl till I come back."

Bran pulls away feeling at once the lack of her touch and, still looking at her, he mounts the worn metal tread into the bus. The driver is already in his seat and the engine is cranking and coughing. Gears clash, and the bus jerks forward with an undulating whine throwing Bran against a chrome bar. He stumbles toward the only empty seat and watches as Mavis's smiling, melancholy face flicks from window to window until it is gone, and he is seized with an anxious feeling akin to sliding down the sheer face of a cliff. He sits down on a narrow bench, knees braced against the back of the seat in front, his pack perched on his lap. As the bus bounces through the town gate and on to the familiar road ahead he begins to savor the unexpected. It is the familiar pre-game anticipation. He isn't sure how, but his innate confidence tells him that he will do what he has to do.

—2—

Nearly every seat in the bus is taken by farmers in blue workshirts, shoulder to shoulder with migrant workers and road-worn, long- distance travelers in rumpled clothes. The baggage rack is stuffed and overflowing, and the floor is strewn with bundles wrapped in brown paper or burlap cloth, shabby suitcases, and even an open weave basket confining two agitated white chickens. Even the dusty air is full, the rancid smell of poultry mingling with sweat and the stench of gasoline exhaust.

Bran looks out of the dusty windows at blurred but still familiar landmarks as the bus lurches along and he sees ahead the place where Ragnar found him. The stone that marks his mother's grave is the boundary of his known world. Beyond it, the trees, rocks, and stream-beds would tell him nothing and he looks back feeling a sense of loss and wanting to cling as long as he can to the familiar.

The man next to him is slumped in a doze, someone behind him breaks into a loose cough, and a baby begins an ear-piercing cry. They pass an old man in a tattered coat, a bed roll slung over his shoulder, stumbling along the road and he recalls four blind people he'd once seen walking on the highway, hand in hand;

literally the blind leading the blind, their heads tilted strangely up, as if to follow the sun. Nothing he could do on this trip would be half as difficult as that. All they had was a white stick while he has his eyes and his wits. Bran looks at the watch that Thule, the head of the Counsel, had given him and he realizes that they have already traveled for half an hour.

He must remember to wind the watch. Thule rang the bell at dawn and Leah rang it before meals. Life's flow was even, the rhythm steady. Long summer days spent in mountain pastures with the sheep; in the spring, the cultivation of the vegetable garden with its high, mulch-rich beds; short, languid winter days with night poised behind the ridge, and long nights spent in the warm kitchen with Leah, Mavis, and Peter, or in the warmth of their own bed with the wind tearing at the corner of their cabin. Whatever happened has happened many times before. Even mishaps, like the attacks of starved coyotes on the sheep, was anticipated.

He thinks of the people of the Glade, outwardly gentle, committed to a non-violent way of life, safe in their isolated valley from all but nature's harsh indifference. Not that there weren't grievances, grudges; but these are aired at public meetings, rituals that somehow managed to clean the dirt out of people's wounds. Bran looks at the man next to him and wonders if he could be trusted, something that never came to mind at the Glade. At the Glade a person always knew the other's strengths and weaknesses. He remembers Leah's advice as she gave him a goodbye bear-hug and a wet kiss tasting of soup. "Don't trust strangers." The rocking, the constant vibration combined with the little sleep of the night before makes him drowsy. At first, he fights it off until he wraps his arms around his pack and slides into a doze, broken occasionally by the sharp sway of the bus and the squeal of brakes.

A wheedling, nasal voice close to his ear brings him fully awake. The man next to him is slight and round-shouldered. He has a long thin nose and shrewd dark eyes that remind Bran of a crow. He grins, displaying long yellow teeth and runs a delicate hand over the stubble of his wrinkled cheek. With his bright, feverish eyes glued to Bran he says, "I had no time to buy food in Templeton having been up late the night before owing to my performance and overslept as a consequence thereof." Bran nods, not completely understanding his peculiar language, and wonders why the man is telling him this. "I thought that you might have a few morsels to spare for which I would gladly pay," the man continues as he pinches his nose and opens his palm to reveal two quarters. He snaps the fingers of his other hand, and two more quarters appear in his palm. Bran looks on fascinated, never having seen human hands move so quickly and with such grace. His eyes on Bran, the man repeats his tricks all the while saying, "Magic, transmigration, concatenation, transmogrification, tintinnabulation, confabulation, the science of necromancy passed from generation to generation from the Druids down to this very time in which we live." Bran stares at the man's hands but says nothing and the man adds, "Alas, a quarter is indigestible, lacking basic nutrition, tender though it may be."

Not expecting to be paid, Bran pulls a small link of deer sausage out of the side pocket of the pack and hands it to his neighbor who takes it between thumb and forefinger, rolls it to his palm and with a flick of his wrist makes it disappear only to be seen a moment later clutched in his teeth like a cigar. Between chewing, he announces with an officious tone, "I am, as should be obvious, Jonah Wells, prestidigitator, although you may already recognize me from my performance in the Variety Show last evening, the cause of my late hours."

He is about to say no, when the bus lurches more than usual throwing him against Jonah and, before they can adjust to the roll, it swings back in the other direction throwing him hard against the arm of the seat. A baby's terrified cry is heard over the squeal of tires and screech of brakes as the bus, gaining speed in its descent, tilts wildly from one curve to another. Bran looks forward, sees the driver spinning the wheel and he realizes with welling fear that the bus has lost its brakes.

Packages shift and hurl out of the baggage rack and fall on the passengers. The basket housing the chickens splits open as it topples over and the white birds flap up to the ceiling only to drop to the floor. Passengers grip seat arms and backs and some scream. Bran looks at his companion and sees that his eyes are wide with terror as the bus skids across the gravel on the edge of the road, teeters indecisively for a moment before tumbling over the rock-strewn edge. The bus slides down the steep embankment on its side, scraping over rocks with a tearing shower of sparks, shoving loose rock ahead of it, and snapping young trees. Passengers on the high side, among them Bran and Jonah, spill out of their seats. Legs and arms twisting and shattering they tumble like clothes in a wash machine amid the boxes and flying packages.

The slide stops at the base of the slope in a grassy meadow. Bran is wedged between Jonah, the seat across the aisle, and the sharp edge of a box. He feels a stabbing pain in his shoulder, and he fights off losing consciousness only to be overcome by nausea. The only possible exit, a row of windows, is now the ceiling reached by a ladder with only one rung, the aisle arm rest. Screams, moans, and angry curses resound as people blindly tear and wrench at each other to get free. Mangled words float above the anguished voices, and he hears a woman crying, "My baby!"

Bran pushes the box aside, struggles to his feet and looks around. People are climbing toward the windows, shoving the weak aside. Bran shouts, "Stay in your place or nobody will get out!"

At the rear, a thin woman is hammering the window marked "Emergency Exit" with her bare fist. Jonah is standing on the seat arm struggling to open a jammed window. "Somebody get me something to break this window, before the bus catches fire!" Jonah shouts as he wrestles with the handles. Bran wrenches forward intending to help until he feels the pain and sees white flashing spots. As his eyes focus he sees that a farmer in faded jeans, his peaked cap still on his head, is clinging to the driver's seat and looking for tools but the driver, slumped forward, his arm twisted into the wheel, is in the way.

A window near the center of the bus shatters and for a moment the cries of the injured stop as repeated blows of a rock wielded by a small, determined hand breaks out the remaining glass. Then a head covered with walnut brown hair thrusts through the jagged frame and Bran recognizes Ephus' searching round eyes and tapered face. At that moment a pair of ham-like arms covered with black hair pushes Ephus back and a bullet-headed man jams his thick torso into the window and becomes wedged. Gasping as the sharp edges of glass cut into his stomach and arms, he forces his way through and escapes. "The emergency window is open!" a woman shouts and some of the pushing is channeled to the rear. Bran looks behind him and sees that a man, long faced and spare, is wedged in his seat against a flabby woman in a pale blue dress. Her head is pitched at an angle, blood trickles out of her mouth and her eyes are locked in an agonized stare.

"Bran?" He hears Ephus' high-pitched voice from the side of the bus next to the window.

"It's OK," Bran shouts back and with his free arm and good shoulder, he forces the seat back to help the man. As the man pulls around him, he is relieved to see his pack on the floor under the seat next to the legs of the woman with the broken neck. He picks it up and tries with his free arm to help people untangle themselves from seats and baggage as he moves toward the broken window. "Everybody will get out," he says. Two uninjured men perched on seat arms just in front and behind the broken window steady and shove as singly, the passengers move through it, cutting themselves on the jagged glass.

Helping as much as he is able, Bran finally reaches the window. Steeled against the pain of wedging his injured shoulder through the tight opening, he pulls himself out onto the side of the bus, takes his pack from one of the men, and sits down next to Ephus waiting for the pain to subside. "How in hell did you get here?" he asks the boy.

"Same as you. I waited for the bus, and I jumped on the ladder where the bus almost stops where the road fell down. You know the place."

Bran shakes his head admiring the boy's tenacity. "Why?"

"I told you I was going with you,"

"I guess I ought to thank you." Ephus, seeing the gratitude in Bran's expression, breaks into an open-mouthed grin exposing his oversized front teeth. Bran looks up at the path of the bus, scraped clean of rocks and shrubs, strewn with the broken crates and bundles that had been stacked on the roof. The bullet-headed man is already climbing up the slope to the road while others either stand in pairs or alone looking stunned and confused or sit on the ground clutching injured parts of their bodies.

"How did you keep from getting killed?"

"I grabbed one of them bundles on the roof and jumped clear as the bus went over."

A woman appears in the window, clinging to her limp baby its head gashed and bloody. She stares out through blind swollen eyes and freezes, not hearing the people inside coaxing her to move. With his good arm, Bran gently touches her shoulder. He looks into her eyes trying to reach her and say, "Take my arm. I'll help." She stares at him, her eyes come alive, and she begins to move forward. After the woman has passed through the window, someone inside hands Bran a small box with a red cross painted on it. He gives it to Ephus and climbs along the side to the rear and lowers himself across the roof ladder to the ground. Ephus jumps down as Bran looks around and wonders what to do. He sees Jonah standing near a pile of soft bundles and goes to him. "Maybe somebody can use this," Bran says, handing him the first-aid kit.

Jonah opens it and paws among the rolls of bandage, finds a bottle and puts it in his pocket saying, "This might do some good," but he makes no move to help anyone.

Bran is about to say something to Ephus when he hears a pop like a firecracker. A tall man in a red quilted jacket with a pistol held in his hand is looking down at another man as he staggers back and falls, clutching his arm. At first Bran doesn't comprehend. He had been told the world beyond the Glade is violent and treacherous, but he hadn't expected to see it so suddenly.

"We better git," Ephus says as he disappears around the corner of the bus. The man looks around, the pistol held loosely in his hand. Is it simply two enemies whose dispute has reached a climax under the pressure of the accident, or have they been fighting over possession of the box next to the wounded man? The one with the gun looks his way and Bran thinks of the money in the pack slung across his good shoulder. He can't take the chance that the man is a thief. As the man takes a step toward the bus, Bran backs behind it and runs toward the trees, half blinded by the pain in his shoulder.

—3—

Bran reaches the screen of trees and slides to the ground gasping from the pain. He leans back against a tree trunk and tries to decide what to do next. He could try to reach the next town and find a doctor. He can't go back to the Glade. It is already too far. Movement in the bushes near him brings him out of his thoughts. Drawing his hunting knife out of its sheath, he flattens against the tree trunk. The rustling stops and he is relieved to hear Ephus call his name. Bran comes out from behind the tree and sees the boy. Jonah's timorous profile immediately appears from behind another tree. Before they can say anything, they are startled by another shot coming from the meadow.

Bran flicks his thumb, and they move through the bushes down a slope which grows increasingly steep until Bran digs his heels into the soft soil and mulch to break his speed. Ephus moves ahead springing down the slope like a goat. At the bottom, Bran collapses against a tree next to a nearly dry stream-bed and bites his lip against the pain in his shoulder. He looks up and sees Jonah descending cautiously but with surprising agility.

"Thought I'd break my neck," says Jonah as he slides the final yard and dusts himself off from the shoulders of his worn, faded black jacket down to his rumpled grey pants. "We seem to have strayed from the beaten path as they say," says Jonah with a gloomy frown deepening the creases in his forehead. "I heard the shot, saw you run, and followed." Bran looks at Ephus, who is kicking at pebbles and scrutinizing Jonah through narrowed eyes.

"You look like you've got some pain," says Jonah.

"It's pretty bad. If you're a real magician maybe you can make it disappear."

Bran meant that as a joke but Jonah chewed his lips and seemed to take it seriously. "Maybe I can."

"You know something about slipped joints?

"Could be," says Jonah and he tentatively takes hold of Bran's arm and probes the injured area with his fingers. "We'll have that back in place before you can recite the Lord's Prayer. You a religious man, Bran? Well, if you are, then pray that I know what I'm doing. Sure wish we had half a pint of alcohol, though."

"What for?" asks Bran breathing hard as Jonah continues to feel the shoulder. "Half for you for the pain and the rest for me to steady my nerves." Jonah says, chewing his narrow lips.

"You know what you're doing?"

The comment provokes a look, at once sober and whimsical, and Jonah replies in a stage-deepened voice, "My boy, it's not a proper question at this time. You have no choice. I am your only hope."

Bran stares at him for a moment then leans back against the trunk of the tree. For the first time Jonah looks at Ephus, and as he kneels beside Bran, he says in a commanding voice, "Get the man a stick."

"What kinda stick?"

"One to bite down on."

Ephus finds a stick and gives it to Bran. Before Bran has it in his mouth, Jonah, with sure rapid movements and strength, seizes Bran's arm, pulls, twists, and returns the joint to its socket with a crackle of cartilage. Bran sees flashes of light. When his eyes focus he sees Ephus looking worried. Next to him Jonah stands, hunched over like a crow, biting a fingernail as though nothing unusual has happened. "Better?"

"You did it," Bran says feeling relieved despite the pulsing ache.

"Did I?" asks Jonah looking both incredulous and pleased with himself. "You're white as a sheet. Lie back and rest. We've got no place to go." Bran lies back using his pack as a pillow. Jonah sits down beside him while Ephus meanders along the stream, his eyes shifting from place to place like an animal foraging for food, repeatedly looking back toward Bran as if to reassure himself that he is still there.

A single cascade of light falling through the canopy of a bay tree catches Bran's attention and he breaths the still, dry, late-summer air and reads its yielding signs. Only the merest trickle of water, a stranger to the stream bed finding its unfamiliar way, reminds him that rain has fallen that week. It is serene, peaceful like the Glade, yet just above are the injured and a man who is not afraid to kill, he thinks.

Through half shut eyes, Bran watches Jonah clean his nails with a pocket knife. "Why don't you take a little rest," Jonah says without looking up. Maybe Leah is wrong about strangers, at least this one, Bran thinks as he looks at the man's deeply lined face. He looks a little like Noah, one of the Council members and is about the same age. His eyes close and drifting in a current of fatigue, Bran sees the Council seated in the undulant light of the Elder's fire. Thule, stout and bald, is splayed uncomfortably on a log. Next to him is Noah, the spare shepherd who seldom spoke an unnecessary word. Micah the head gardener, the third Council member, a wiry man with a thick red nose and glasses is sitting on the end of the log, hunched over and whittling a twig with his pocketknife. Spare and erect as a fir tree, the Elder stands before them, his white hair unruly, dressed in course homespun loose pants and shirt, a sheep skin cape flung over his shoulders against the night chill. They are listening as Thule speaks in his halting way of the danger to the Glade.

Something called the Standard Company has applied for the right to operate the mine on the ridge above the Glade. Unless their community perfected its claim by obtaining the patent to the land by the end of the month, Standard would have the mine and their land with it. Almost $200,000 New Dollars is needed to obtain the patent but living on what they grew and made themselves, they are lucky to put together a tenth of that.

Bran asked why they hadn't secured their right to the land before and the Elder explained that at the time of the general land distribution the people of the Glade had refused to pay for a patent to the land choosing on principle to be outlaws, to live outside the law and its protection. But their leader, Ragnar, had secretly set the money aside and passed it to the Elder at his death. With that revelation the Elder gave Thule a roll of Old

Dollars in a leather pouch, and he urged, if not commanded, the Council to send Bran south to Irvine to register the patent.

How foolish they had been, thought Bran, to wait until it was almost too late. What use is a principle if it kept you from doing what is best for you? It is a shoe with a hole in it he mused and with his eyes closed, his senses melted by unguent sunlight falling through the branches, he slips into a doze. A gentle prodding of his good arm brings Bran out of a deep sleep, and he sees Ephus's smooth, tapered face and Jonah's deeply creased face, bending over him looking impatient and expectant.

"We'll need to find shelter for the night," says Jonah. Bran yawns, measures the pain in his shoulder and sits up. He takes some sausage out of his pack and divides it between them. Jonah chews enthusiastically and looks gratefully at Bran, reminding him of his dog, Caleb.

"What's in it? Deer?" he asks and then confesses that he has, in his lifetime eaten gopher, muskrat, horse, dog, and cat during the Great Parch. Ephus wrinkles his upper lip in disgust.

"Time to move on," says Bran squinting into the slanting rays of the sun. He knew the bus schedules and there was no point in going back to the road and certainly not in the vicinity of the accident. Ephus looks expectant and Bran smiles down at him. "Ephus, why don't you try and get us to some shelter. Tomorrow we can get back to the road and flag down a bus." His mobile face brightens and Ephus immediately starts picking his way along the rocky stream's edge crossing bars of light and shadow.

"Hope he knows where he's going," says Jonah, his voice nasal and anxious.

"Better than a hound," says Bran and he thinks back on the first time he'd seen Ephus. There had always been something different about him. A lively intelligence shown from his bright eyes, and despite his circumstances, there was something sure about him as though, fragile as his existence was, he somehow managed to get along. Bran had observed him, deftly stealing food from farmers on market days.

It had taken six months before he had agreed to come to the Glade with Bran. Even after sharing food with him, talking gently, gradually winning his confidence, it was the promise of a ride on Morningstar, as much as anything, that had impelled Ephus to come with him. Bran recalled his surprise at the child's cleanliness the day he brought him back to the Glade. He bathed in cold streams, even washed his clothes, but he was suspicious of soap. And he continued to sleep out of doors, even on cold nights, only compromising on the night of the first rain when Bran had gotten up to find him asleep just inside the door of the cabin back- to- back with Caleb, the dog.

"You travel pretty light," says Bran looking at Jonah's little satchel.

"Everything I need; razor, clean shirt, underwear, and my tricks."

"What have you got in the way of tricks?"

"Since my trunk was destroyed in a fire, I just carry basic magician's tools; a wand, some handkerchiefs, and playing cards. I also read minds when the spirit moves me."

Mavis's ability to intuit danger comes to mind and a ripple of fear runs through him at the thought that Jonah might learn of his money. They continue along the stream bed as the shadows fade and color bleeds from the leaves. High above the tree- line in the western sky the lucid white afterglow slowly dies until at last they find themselves in the darkness of a cave. They stumble a lot and Bran is glad of Ephus's ability. He has no idea how far they have drifted from the course of the road but is satisfied that their path is taking them in the right direction.

Bran is thinking about Mavis, wondering what she is doing when he realizes that Ephus isn't in front of him anymore. He stops and Jonah soon comes up short behind him. Within a minute or so Ephus returns to announce that he has come on a cache of aluminum cans, and he wants to take some of them. "I can get good money for them," Ephus says.

It would compensate the boy for his help, Bran reasons as they flatten the cans and stuff them into his poncho its ends tied together into a pack. He is amazed that Ephus had spotted them in the darkness. At that moment Bran thinks that he could have no better companions than a magician and healer and a child that sees in the dark.

Ephus offers to give Jonah a share if he carries the bulky pack and Bran is surprised when Jonah agrees. They go on, Ephus in the lead and Jonah clanging behind like a belled goat. Before they have gone very far, Ephus stops again, this time to announce that he has discovered a path used by people. "The path hasta go to a cabin," says Ephus having gotten down on his hands and knees to examine the ground.

"How do you know?" asks Jonah.

"I kin feel the outline of a heel of a shoe in the ground."

They had walked for hours, and Bran had no idea how soon they would find the next town. If the trace led to a cabin at least they might find out how best to get to a town in the morning. "Let's try it out," Bran says. "Are you game, Jonah?"

"I hope not," Jonah replies as he falls in behind Bran. It is even darker under the trees, but it is as if Ephus's eyes have shifted to the soles of his feet, for he moves along steadily and without a sound. They have gone about 50 yards when Bran hears Jonah stumble to the ground with a loud clatter of metal and a hysterical cry. He turns back and finds the man picking himself up to the clash of the cans. As Bran gives him his good hand, Jonah whispers in a shaking voice, "Something pushed me; an animal."

"It must have run off, scared by the noise of the cans," he says, to humor Jonah, assuming that he had simply stumbled on a root. So he thinks at least until he hears a crackling of branches and sees a ghostly shape of something. Jonah must have heard it too for his shaking is so violent that the cans continuously rattle an alarm. Before Bran can push Jonah in front of him two dogs begin a menacing, staccato alarm and Bran thinks at least we've found a place to ask directions.

They catch up with Ephus and find him standing in front of a barbed wire fence listening to the angry barking. Again, they hear the crackling of an animal in the dense branches and Bran turns toward the sound, unsure what to expect. For the second time he draws his knife out of the leather sheath. Jonah's attacker appears, a sanguine looking goat no doubt wondering how someone came to be on the path as it returned home from a night of foraging.

A yellow light, barely stronger than a single match, lit a doorway beyond the fence and another shape as white as the goat, but human, approaches them calling, "Hush up, Clarence, Opal! It's only Corny, the goat." The dogs pay no attention to her and keep up their excited clamor feeding on each other's enthusiasm. It is an old woman's voice, shrill and quavering, and hearing it Bran is reassured. Ephus has led them down the right path.

Jonah, in his dulcet, theatrical voice, says, "Madame, take pity on three injured, lost victims of a bus accident."

"Who's that?" the woman says, a startled exclamation.

Bran adds in a calm and simple way, "Can you tell us how to get to the nearest town? We got lost running away from some thieves."

After a pause she says, "You're not thieves yourselves, are you? If you are, you should know that there's a loaded shotgun pointed at you." Her tone is earnest but steady, considering that she is an old woman facing two strange men. The flickering yellow light floats closer, and he sees what looks like the butt of a rifle.

"We're not thieves, ma'am. I'm a farmer from up in the Forest Service Enclave with an injured shoulder. And there's an old man and a boy with me."

"You haven't seen a goat out there, have you?" The voice is lower now. "And get your hands up all the same until I can get a look at you."

"I can't raise my arm."

"Put up whatever you can and no tricks." The floating light comes to the fence, and they see a slight old woman in a white flannel gown, fine grey hair tied but floating around a pinched and withered face of a doll made from a dried apple. She squints across the fence at them as the dogs, having grown tired of the barking, stop after one more half -hearted exclamation.

"Just tell us the way to the next village," Bran says, his voice gentle and persuasive.

"It won't do you any good to go there," she says in a peevish way. "You can come in here and rest if you like. The gate's on your right. And let the goat in please." They follow her to a cabin lit by the feeble light of a dying fire. An old man, emaciated, with a long face, the bones barely covered by dry skin, is dozing in a crude rocking chair beside the stone hearth.

Once they are inside the door the woman's demeanor softens. She smiles warmly and pays special attention to Ephus who responds with his usual suspicious reserve. Without asking, she serves them fresh bread, goat cheese, blackberry preserves, and herb tea. When they are all seated around the crude table on simple ladder back chairs she pulls a stool out of the corner, sits down opposite her husband and watches them hunch over their food, accepting the occasional quick glance of appreciation with a gentle, nostalgic expression.

After eating, Ephus looks around the room, spots an empty corner, goes to it and lies down on the floor, curling up like a dog. The woman looks at her husband, his head nodding against his chest. She puts three small logs on the fire, pokes the embers with a stick until it blazes throwing swaying shadows around the walls.

"I've almost forgotten how to talk to guests. We see so few people anymore." Untethered, her tongue gambols from garden seeds to the depth of winter frost. Memories gush out of her. She speaks in different tones like music, sometimes with wrenching emotion, at other times with a leaf-light nostalgia, the memory of a bitter smile reflecting in her eyes. Caught up in her feeling, even when he doesn't understand the things she is describing, Bran listens attentively. A schoolteacher, she had lived with her husband, an insurance broker, and their two children, a boy and a girl, in a town called Hayward on the San Francisco Bay. While her husband nods in his chair and Jonah cracks and gnaws on chestnuts from her tree, she speaks of the aftermath of the

Great Parch when everything stopped, seemed to start up again then slowly stopped for good.

She stops to poke the fire, put a blanket around her husband and continues. The towns around the Bay took years to die. Everything that happened affected everyone else. People were out of work, homeowners defaulted in their loans, people couldn't afford to buy new clothes, even gasoline for their car. Businesses closed. There wasn't enough tax revenue to provide services. Schools closed, fire stations, police stations, were reduced to skeleton staffs, roads went unrepaired, streetlights burned out and were not replaced, sewers broke down and drainage overflowed into streets. Row after row of stores abandoned by tenant and landlord alike were boarded up, squatted in by the homeless, or burned.

"We probably would have come through it, but the drought finished us," she says. It affected not only California but the Plains States. At first food became more and more expensive, then meat began to disappear from the markets, and finally even grains became hard to get. Eventually even water was rationed by increasing the price. Everyone had a vegetable garden in their back yards, and many fenced their front yards as well and people didn't bathe very much, it wasted too much water."

For Bran, the stories were like exploring a cave for the first time with a strong light. He resented that young people at the Glade hadn't been told more. The Glade has no books except for a few dealing with the most practical matters; first aid and medicine, plant and animal diseases, and natural remedies. True to his pragmatism, Ragnar believed that the world suffered from too much education and too little understanding. "I never met a fox that could read or a scholar who could snare a rabbit," he would say. He taught them only what people needed to survive. Bran yawns and looks across the room at the shadows from the fire. Maybe Ragnar has taken pragmatism too far. Bran would have liked to have known more about the world if only to understand why the people of the Glade had given up on it. Idle thoughts won't pluck the chicken. The saying, also Ragnar's, came to him. If tomorrow is like today, he will need a good rest. He can't undo what has happened, but he can get a good night's sleep. That much is in his power. He lies down near Ephus, puts his pack under his head and pulls his poncho over him.

The old woman sets the shotgun down on the floor beside her bed. She lies back and covers herself with a thick patch-work quilt. There is no sound but the occasional snap of the collapsing fire. Only a few hours ago he had been with Mavis. So much has happened in one day.

THE SECOND DAY

—1—

The austere light and sharp chill of an autumn morning awakens Bran. For just a moment it seems like just another day, then the throbbing of his stiff and aching shoulder brings back yesterday. Refreshed by his usual sound sleep, he sits up, stretches, tries to flex his shoulder, and lets his mind drift back to his morning routine at the Glade. Through the window he sees Ephus engaged in a tug-of-war with one of the dogs, a long-haired black Shepherd, and a warm feeling comes over him. He is not alone after all and his companion is well adapted to the hazards of the road.

The old woman is up too, dressed in bib overalls so patched that none of the original material shows. She is bent over the table mixing batter for cornbread. A lively fire is crackling in the hearth and Bran goes to it and warms himself breathing the moist air from the pot of water just beginning to steam. The old man gets up from the rocking chair and shuffles to the door on flat scraping feet, his eyes focused on something distant yet within. The woman serves them goat cheese, fresh corn bread spread with blackberry jam and honey, and herb tea. When Bran asks the distance and direction to the main road, she raises both hands and drops them toward him. "It's a long way. You must have come in a big circle from the accident." Then she gives them directions to the next compound and even insists that they take food with them.

"Is it far from the main road down to the Valley?" Bran asks.

"Very far. But it's still the shortest way unless you're part mountain goat."

On the way to the gate, Bran admires the garden, still bright with dew, the raised beds mulched for the frost. Sentinel dahlias, gaudy red and orange, and sunburst chrysanthemums cluster bravely, taking what they can from the diluted autumn sunlight.

The old woman looks on with suspicion as Ephus shoulders the rattling cans "What on earth is that?"

"Just some old metal cans," he replies, hoisting them higher so that they clear the ground.

"The things people take a fancy to," she mutters as she watches them pass from the order of her garden to the wild thicket that surrounds it. She waves and the gate closes with a click of the latch. The wispy grey top of her head is visible over the fence and Bran wonders if they would meet many others as hospitable. The forest cover closes around him he hears the goat bleat and realizes that he didn't even get the woman's name.

They descend a worn path among fir and tan oak. Shrubs, their foliage shriveled and brown, overhang the path and brush against them, dropping seed on their clothes. They plunge through fields of wan morning light, solid with the suspended dust of autumn. Mid-morning the tall trees yield to faded, roll-ing rye grass and gnarled umbrellas of ancient live oak. Coming to the crest of a hill they see below a dense cluster of shake roofs surrounded by geometric fields evenly striated to the edge of a double chain link fence. Except for the pointed spire of a church, the roofs are uniform, each pitch rising to the same peak. A narrow, paved road runs the length of the small valley and passes a gate in the fence before it climbs a narrow switch-back through a grove of oak to the cusp of the far ridge.

They stop and Bran lies down in the dry grass, stretches out his good arm, and stares up at the uniform blue of the sky. He lets his mind soar, blocking Jonah's complaints of the blisters on his feet and the awkward shifting of the cans which he has carried most of the way. Then he stands, conscious of the pain in his shoulder, slings his pack over his good arm, and says, "At least we don't have to be afraid of rattle snakes with all that noise."

"I'm sick of carrying them. Maybe somebody down there wants to buy them," Jonah says, wiping the sweat off his forehead with the back of his free hand.

"Even better if we could hitch a ride to the main road," Bran says, already resigned to losing a second day. Ephus looks at both with what might be contempt and strides down a path etched into the faded golden hillside. Within ten minutes the three of them are following a track along the perimeter fence. Bran gazes at the neat rows and the people scattered among them, their backs bent over short-handled hoes. He focuses on an orchard at the other end of the compound and identifies expertly pruned apple, peach, apricot, and walnut trees. As they approach the convergence of the field with the houses, a German Shephard runs towards them and stares suspiciously through the fence. Ahead is a small cemetery enclosed by a low, split-rail fence. Mourners are huddled about a fresh-dug grave in the shadow of three yew trees.

Just outside the cemetery a man is playing a sorrowful tune on a violin. Judging by his ragged dress he is an itinerant musician; one of many who pass from town to town, entertaining in marketplaces or cafes. A tall man, the musician has a commanding presence—at least it seemed so to Bran. Yet his features are soft, his cheeks are round as is his chin, and the polished skin, as dark as an old walnut chair seat, belies the graying, tightly curled hair. His eyes are round, their color is a striking lapis blue set in old ivory and they seem, both because of their shape and contrast to the dark skin, to be filled with wonder if not naiveté. The violin looks like a toy in his large hands and as he plays, he gazes down his cheeks and works his fleshy lips as though he were speaking to the instrument.

The ceremony ends as they draw close, and they wait as the mourners leave the graveyard in twos and threes and straggle past the violinist toward the gate. Although he continues to play and his grey woolen cap is open on the ground in front of him, no one, not even the tearful widow, leave him any money. When the last of them has passed, he stops playing in the middle of his dirge and wrapping the violin in a soft brown cloth, he places it in a battered case.

Ephus walks up to him and gawks at his size and appearance. "You play good."

The man grins showing large white teeth and says, "I hate to play funeral music but I knew the man that died." Momentary sadness steals across his face. "He was a good man." Then he looks up, bright as before, and adds, "No cheating death."

Bran stares at him with unconcealed curiosity. Only the second Black person Bran has ever seen. The first was Sam, an elderly woodworker in Templeton, who looked to Bran like he'd been carved out of wood himself.

Muttering something, Jonah shrugs, picks up the pack of cans, and heads for the town gate. The stranger watches him with a bemused shake of his head. Offering his massive hand he introduces himself. "Nikanor Best." As they catch up with Jonah, the fiddler explains that he has spent the night here but is on his way to Fresno.

The sign over the wooden gateposts announce in wrought-iron letters, "Kiwanis C Security Community Faith". The way in is blocked by a red and white striped pipe that can be raised or lowered by a guard. A thin man in a dark blue shirt and baggy pants is leaning against his hut, noisily eating a ripe peach, and studiously ignoring all four of them.

Ephus, as unobtrusive as a black cat in a shadow, walks around the group and sidles into the guard's hut, remaining about as long as a raccoon might pause at the door of a kitchen. Before the exchange with the guard has concluded, he is back again standing beside Bran peering up at the guard, his blank expression deceptively indifferent to the workings of the adult world.

"Do you know how long it'll take to get to the main road?" Bran asks.

"Couple hours," says Nikanor. "If you don't mind the company, I'll walk along with you."

"You know anything about the buses from Fresno south to Los Angeles?"

Nikanor looks at him with interest. "Stage buses or direct?"

"Direct."

"About every six hours."

He is relieved to hear this and stops being concerned about the loss of two days. There is still plenty of time if nothing more goes wrong. Their backs turned on the town they walk along the side of the road doing their best to keep up with Nikanor's long stride. After 100 or so yards Bran notices Ephus examining something that gleams. Reflexively aware of Bran's attention Ephus stuffs the object into his pocket, as Bran asks, "What've you got there Ephus?"

"Just a stone I picked up on the road."

"It looked like metal. Can I see it?"

"No!" says Ephus jumping out of Bran's reach.

Nikanor looks down at him, a tolerant smile creasing the corners of his blue eyes, and says, "He made a little trip into that guard booth while Jonah here was negotiating. I suspect he picked himself up a souvenir of the hospitality of the town."

Bran presses his lips together and looks down at Ephus with a mixture of severity and humor. "You'll never mend your ways, it seems." Ephus returns a contemptuous stare and says, "If I didn't take stuff I'd be dead."

Bran turns his head away thinking that Ephus is probably right about his own life at least. He considered himself fortunate to have been taken off of the harsh road before he had learned its rules.

"The boy's a first-rate thief," says Jonah. "With a good teacher to show him the fine points he'd go right to the top, no doubt about it."

"Sort of the same as being a pres... whatever you call yourself?" asks Bran.

"Just the opposite," says Jonah without a pause. "I make things appear out of nowhere; that's a lot harder let me tell you." And with that introduction the conversation shifts to the illusion of magic and Ephus is left to fall behind and furtively examine his stolen treasure.

With Jonah lagging behind burdened by the cans, they soon leave the road and hike up the neck of the valley toward the western ridge. As they walk Nikanor and Bran get acquainted although neither tells the other much about himself. Nikanor claims to be from Detroit, "a free city like Fresno." Bran listens but is reluctant to show his ignorance with too many questions. For his part Bran only says that he is a farmer on his way to Fresno to arrange for the sale of some cattle.

"Where'd you get the name Bran?" asks Nikanor.

"When they found me on the road all I had was a doll made out of a corn husk. Ragnar the one that found me, named me after the corn God."

"It's a good name for a farmer."

Bran looked at him and smiled. "It's easy to spell."

The ascent grows steeper and the switchbacks in the path pass through groves of live oak yielding to sparse fir and spruce until they reach the saddle. The ridge falls like the sides of a bowl into a wide, mutilated valley. Earth slides and erosion have taken great bites out of the hills leaving pocks from which protrude the torn muscle and bone of the earth. Skeletons of fallen trees, their roots twisted in anguish, lay upturned on the slopes or in great tangles. In the notch of the valley a river, yellow with mud, moves like sludge over the surface of its stone and silt- filled bed, watched over by isolated laurels and cottonwoods. To Bran it is like discovering a body abandoned and decaying by the road. Nikanor explains that the forest was clear-cut after the Parch to provide housing for the homeless and never replanted.

Bran tries not to look at the valley as he divides the remains of the corn bread and most of the sausage with his companions. While they eat, Jonah recovers his spirits enough to demonstrate some sleight of hand and even tries to teach Ephus a simple trick with a pebble. After a little rest they walk along a path clinging to the ridge, and before long come to the main highway.

Jonah dumps the cans with the now familiar clatter as Nikanor tells them that they are no more than seven miles from the Inspection Station that marks the border between the Sierra District administered by the Forest Service and the Valley District. "The Agriculture Department might not let you in unless you have travel documents," says Nikanor.

Bran acknowledges that he doesn't have any. "It makes no never mind," says Jonah. "Just spread a little butter on the inspector's bread." Bran looks perplexed at that.

"A bribe. All the same, I always take the way of the smugglers," says Nikanor. "No waiting and you never know what will turn up on their computer. I saw them stop a child hardly bigger than Ephus because the computer told them that he was an escaped felon."

"Maybe he was," says Jonah and he bares his yellow, rodent teeth in a loose lipped grin.

"Something coming," says Ephus. Soon they all heard the throaty exhaust of heavy diesel engines and a convoy of four mud-colored Army trucks, the Golden Bear of the California Republic outlined on their doors, passes, their heavy lug tires whining. Nikanor stiffens for a moment and relaxes as the blue smoke from the exhaust envelopes them.

They continue down the road toward a trail that, according to Nikanor, makes a wide loop around the Inspection Station. How lucky to have met Nikanor, Bran thinks, and he wonders, what would have happened if he had simply blundered into the Inspection Station expecting to obtain transit documents into the next district.

They had walked about a mile when Ephus announces that a horse is approaching. Before long a heavy sorrel work horse, pulling a four-wheel rubber tired wagon, plods around a bend. A farmer has the reins, but he is slouched over and might even be asleep. Before the wagon comes abreast of them Jonah calls out, "Could we get a ride down the road?"

"It's empty," says the farmer stopping the horse. With a slight shift of his head, he invites them to climb on. When they are all seated around the edge of the wagon the horse goes on at a slightly faster pace. Eventually, Bran asks him if he is going as far as the Inspection Station.

"Nope,"

They roll along quietly on the rubber tires, bouncing over potholes, listening to the regular clapping of the horse's hooves. Above them the sky is cloudless and the sun, having fallen almost to the horizon, glares straight at them. Bran looks over the edge of the road at the devastated valley for some sign of life and he is seized by a longing for the familiarity of the Glade where the trees still hold the ridges in place. He imagines the crisp herbal fragrance of Mavis, fresh from a wash in the spring. There she is, practicing a dance with several children, hand in hand, her hair rising and falling about her shoulders, the long white skirt flaring and fluting as she leaps.

The wagon halts at the entrance of a dirt road cut into the side of the ridge. As they prepare to climb down, Jonah asks if they might have shelter for the night. Surprisingly, the farmer replies that they are welcome to sleep in the stable. Better than the cold ground, they all agree. Bran eases back against the wagon sides, and as it jars forward, he again concludes that there are a lot of helpful strangers, surely more than he had been led to believe.

Twenty minutes later as the sun slips behind the ridge, they come to a cluster of stucco, tile roofed buildings surrounded by a high yellow wall. They pass through the unmarked gate and enter a garden. Specimen trees line the walls, overlapping to show off the variety of color, texture, and leaf. The beige walls of the buildings are softened by shrubs and leafy vines that in some places wrap tendrils around the windows. At the center of the compound is a large green lawn broken by bright beds of flowers laid out in precise color fields and crossed by winding, gravel paths. Every plant is well tended and pruned to perfection as if in response to some preordained design. Bran is astonished that such a place could exist in the middle of the devastated forest. He stares at the unkempt hair of the farmer, his gray work-shirt, worn through at the collar, as if to confirm that this place is real. The wagon continues around the perimeter of the garden on a gravel drive and Bran sees a plashing fountain, its octagonal basin faced with azure blue tile, and beyond it a white gazebo with a red cupola roof around which are several young girls wearing white tunics gathered at the waist. One girl, long brown hair fanned over her shoulders, is seated on the gazebo steps playing a stringed instrument while the others are singing a lyrical round in three-part harmony. Two more girls are seated on the benches that ring the gazebo, listening and sewing. As with the perfection of the garden, Bran is struck by symmetry of the girls, their limbs long and well formed, their faces different but all lovely as if, like the trees, they have been carefully selected and reared to meet some pre-ordained standard of beauty.

Not far from the gazebo stands a white marble statue of a young woman resembling the ones seated and lounging in the area. Two girls in fact are talking quietly in its shadow, their backs against the statue's base. Their knees are clasped close to their chests, and the skirts of their tunics have fallen back on their thighs revealing long slender legs that somehow call to mind the grace and symmetry of a young deer that he'd once seen as it paused then danced into a screen of foliage. All the beauty he has seen before has been natural; the random seeding of plants around stones lying where they have fallen, the grandeur of a grove of mature firs with bright planes of sunlight filtering through windows in the branches. This place is a jarring new perception to him, and, despite its appeal, he is relieved when the cart rounds a corner and returns him to the familiar utilitarian world of greasy, battered farm implements, weathered doors, and the smell of cow dung piled near the dark entrance of a stable.

Beyond the farm buildings is a more comfortable sight, a noisy game of soccer. "What is this place, a school?" asks Bran and the farmer mutters over his shoulder, "Yep."

The horse stops in front of the stable and the farmer gets down, points toward the back entrance of a two-story stucco building near the open shed and stable, and says, "They'll fix you up with some food and shelter for the night." Without looking at them he begins to unbuckle the horse's harness as they climb down.

A whistle blows and the players leave the field and walk past them in clusters, shrieking and jostling each other. Unlike the young people at the gazebo their hair is cropped short and developing breasts can be seen rising on several of the still heaving chests, while others have the rounding of hips and buttocks of maturing girls. Most of the athletes ignore them but several turn coquettish, if shy, glances toward Bran.

Announced by the clatter of the cans against the door jam, they enter a pantry adjoining a large white-tiled kitchen. Five white-clad cooks and helpers are busy preparing the evening meal, chopping vegetables, and stirring large steaming aluminum pots. Bran and the others just stand and watch, inhaling the smell of cooking meat and the yeasty fragrance of loaves of bread lined up on a table. The workers pay no attention to them until Jonah steps up to a swarthy man who has just stopped dicing tomatoes to push his hair out of his eyes.

"Pardon me," says Jonah with stilted politeness, "we are injured victims of a bus accident brought here by one of your workmen. He suggested that we might have something to eat and a place to stay the night." The man looks at him blankly and says something in a garbled nasal language to another, a round faced man with narrow black eyes and a yellowish skin wearing a hat that looks to Bran like a blanched mushroom.

"Go sit in dining room across hall, table near door," says the man in the chef's hat. "We bring food. Boss say OK, you sleep in barn." The chef looks from one to the other as though he were inspecting a cut of meat. "You better wash first," and he waves his knife in the direction of the pantry.

In the pantry they find a utility sink, lye soap, and towels made of sack cloth. Mindful of his stiff and sore shoulder, Bran scrubs the dust of the road from his hands and thinks how nice it would be to wash in the spring and douse off with hot water in the wooden tub behind the kitchen at the Glade. As usual Ephus refuses the soap. Bran tells him that he smells like a hen-house and, with a defiant look and a flush on his cheeks, Ephus goes outside. Nikanor soon follows looking for a toilet.

"Your young friend, Ephus, is out there in his birthday suit washing down at a tap. Two of those soccer players are having themselves a time watching but he doesn't seem to mind," says Nikanor when he returns.

"He's got nothing to be ashamed of," says Bran amused by Ephus's little escapade. Eventually Ephus comes back looking shiny and self-satisfied, still wearing the same clothes but smelling better.

The dining room is a high-ceilinged hall with long communal tables. They sit down at the table nearest the door to the kitchen. Bran is the first to reach for the basket of still warm bread and they all follow. While they devour the bread, children of various ages, some as young as Ephus, all wearing the same short white tunics, straggle into the dining hall, talking and laughing with animation, filling the place with echoing voices and scraping chair sounds. When nearly all of the tables are filled, including the one next to Bran, someone stands, gives a signal, and the room resounds with a song in three-part harmony in a strange language and an equally unfamiliar melody. Listening to the trained and blended chorus Bran concludes that the place must be a music school. He looks across at Nikanor and says, "Do you know anything about this place?"

Nikanor's eyes range about the room, and he says in a low voice, "I do, yes." Savory lamb stew is soon placed on the table in steaming bowls and Bran and his companions heap their plates and eat. Bent over his plate, Bran has just mopped up the last of the brown gravy with a corner of bread when he realizes that the young woman sitting on his left is talking to him. It is a singular voice; dusty, resonant, and sweet as though it is two voices combined in tight harmony.

"Do you always eat like that?"

He straightens up, turns toward her and quips, "No, only at mealtime." As she chuckles softly, he gets a better look at her. Her hair, muted auburn with red highlights, tumbles in waves about her broad cheeks and falls carelessly to her shoulders. Her eyes, dull blue and almond shaped, are lit with curiosity. Her lips are full except where they turn up at the corners. She observes him studying her and her smile extends until she cuts it off, pressing her full lips together. A coquettish challenge steals into her eyes mingling with unconcealed appreciation of Bran's symmetrical features.

"Would you like some coffee? We have it twice a week," she says, picking up a white china pitcher. Bran nods, although he has never before tasted it owing to the prohibitive cost. As she reaches across him to pour, he catches a glimpse of round breasts nestled in a white halter under her loosely buttoned pale blue shirt. Her eyes pass his with an amused mocking flash. Her hair has fallen over her cheek and she raises a hand with long, slender fingers and brushes it back, a gesture that is both stylized and graceful. Then she introduces herself with just her first name, "June." Bran gives her his own name, and those of his companions, briefly explaining how they have come to be there.

"Do you work here, or are you a student?" he asks, deciding that the coffee is too bitter for him.

She looks at him hesitantly then says carefully, "I'm studying voice. What about you? What do you do?" and he tells her that he is a farmer on his way to Los Angeles. June nods and looks interested.

One of the kitchen help comes to the table to tell them that they can sleep in the stable and he offers to show them the room. "Lead me too it," says Jonah looking at the others. Ephus gets up, takes the last piece of bread, stuffs it into his pocket, and leaves the room, followed immediately by two young girls.

"I guess I'd better get settled myself," says Bran.

June says, "There's no hurry. Let me show you around first." She puts her hand on his forearm to check him and watches as Nikanor and Jonah leave, the latter having first given Bran a theatrical wink. She says confidentially, "The stable isn't a very nice place. I might find you a real bed if you like."

"I'm used to sleeping on a blanket on the ground. But I wouldn't turn a bed down, that and a place to wash, better than that slop sink in the pantry."

"Done." The dining room is beginning to empty and is noisy with clearing plates, echoing conversation and laughter. "Would you mind if we took a little walk first?"

"Sure. I'd like to take a closer look at the garden. Where I come from everything's just the way it comes up out of the ground. I suspect that there are people here that do nothing but care for the flowers and shrubs."

She stands and Bran sees that she is tall, with wide shoulders that taper to narrow hips. Her loose dark blue skirt barely reaches her knees and as she walks ahead of him the skirt's flare reveals long, well-shaped legs. She looks back at him, a mischievous spark in her eyes and says, "You are coming, aren't you?"

They walk the dark paths of the garden as June talks of her curiosity about the world and her desire to eventually leave the school and make a life for herself in one of the cities. Bran listens with one ear, aware of the night fragrances, the growing chill, the dark shapes of the shrubs and flower beds with their abstracted colors, and he wonders what his life would have been had he gone to this school. Comfort and refinement are alien to him. His world is simple and closed. Listening to June, he feels a tug of desire to be something more than a farmer.

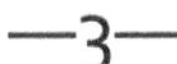

Ten minutes later, not far from the gazebo, between two shrubs, they see two young people pressed together on the ground in motion, their naked shapes glowing silver in the moonlight. As the shapes move, between elbows and arms he sees a fragment of Ephus's profile twisted in pain or ecstasy, and above him, in a panting cadenza, a lithe and nubile girl. Bemused, Bran walks on. There are no sexual inhibitions at the Glade; children are raised among animals and understand from the age of five, if not earlier, what all creatures do to make new life. The sexual act is a celebration of life to the people of the Glade. Still, Ephus is a little young, he thinks.

"That was quick. They hardly left the dining room twenty minutes ago."

"Francine gets right to the point. No beating around the bush," says June, looking over her shoulder with the mildly curious gaze of a passerby who observes two dogs joined together. "Does that bother you?"

"No. Where I came from, sex is the chief function of religion."

"I take it you aren't Christian."

"No, we're Pragmatists."

"Is that supposed to be a joke?"

"No. Ragnar, the man that founded the Glade, our farm, taught that the life cycle is the center of everything, and sex is the center of the life cycle."

"I see," says June turning her face toward him with a glow of understanding. "Pragmatism, as I understand it, is the belief that whatever works is right. How does that get you to a religion that stresses sex?"

"The way Ragnar explained it, a farmer depends on sex for just about everything from increasing his herds to germinating and pollinating plants. It's all sex of one kind or another. So, sex is kind of sacred; a, what's the word, a consecration of life."

"Even if it isn't going to produce more life?"

"Then I guess it's something like practicing for the next day's game," he said, thinking of hyde ball. She gives Bran an enigmatic smile and they walk on quietly for a time.

Suddenly, she stops and turns to face him. "If you like you can have even more than a wash? How would you like a hot bath and a massage?"

"The way I feel, I'd kill for it."

"That won't be necessary." June cocks her head toward him and sweeps a wave of hair out of her eyes. She watches him, her auburn, arched eyebrows raised in anticipation, an indulgent smile playing on her half-open full lips. He responds with a weary nod. A lyrical laugh of pleasure escapes her lips then she quickens her stride and motions with a little scoop of the hand.

Her room is comfortable, luxurious by the austere standards of the Glade. Warm in the light of the oil lamp with its amber shade, it is furnished with a large bed, with room enough for three abreast, Bran observes. Clearly the bed is the most important of the furnishings for it has a covering of downy pastel and half a dozen plump cushions, the feathers of a hundred geese, he thinks. There is a tall-backed rocking chair with a cane seat, a table with a neat array of bottles, perfumes, and cosmetics, and a mirror large enough to contemplate the entire body. The floor is the most astonishing appointment of all covered with a beige carpet so soft that Bran would have enjoyed an adequate night's sleep on it.

He looks at her, sees her bemused expression, and feels a flush come into his cheeks. "Pretty nice." With a flourish of her hand, she lures him toward the bathroom; shining white tile and porcelain with an immaculate white tub. Accustomed to the galvanized washtubs and cold spring water of the Glade, Bran gawks with astonishment. The chrome taps squeal as she turns them and steaming hot water gushes from the faucet.

"It comes from a hot spring. This will relax you, and after I've given you that massage you won't even know you injured your shoulder," says June soothingly. Without asking she begins unbuttoning his shirt and pants.

"I can get that."

"Let me. You've got a bad arm."

Used to the Glade where men and women often bathed together in the stream, he wasn't the least self-conscious about showing his body to a strange woman. Having helped him undress, June appraises his tapered body admiringly. "My but you're a fine specimen," she says. Then with a mock imperious tone and a graceful flourish of her arm she adds, "Now get into that tub slowly so that you don't burn yourself." He plunges a foot into the steaming water and pulls it out again. She shows him how to draw some cold water and leaves the room for a time but not before she has poured some bath salts into the water saying, "This will help relax your muscles."

Slowly, Bran eases himself into the tub and lets it fill around him. Eventually settled down and immersed up to the neck, he feels the soothing heat draw the ache out of his shoulder until every muscle in his body is as limp as a thirsty tomato plant. A blissful daydream of a lazy summer afternoon fills his head until, jolted by sudden anxiety, he looks toward the corner of the bathroom and is reassured that the pack is where he had left it.

The whole trip is worth this moment, he decides, when June comes back wearing nothing but a lustrous one-piece garment; a halter supported by thin shoulder straps cut to a v between her breasts, gathered at the waist and flared to what looks like running shorts except that all of the edges are delicately fluted. Over her right breast is a little red triangle with the letters "SRI" inside it. She has loosely tied her hair behind her head with a blue ribbon and it billows out around her face making a lovely bronze frame for her sun-tanned skin. Seeing her long legs, firm upstanding breasts, and a gentle shy appearance in her eyes, Bran feels a stirring that even the relaxing hot water doesn't inhibit.

"You look about as content as a nursing calf."

"And just as helpless. I'm so weak I could be knocked over by a bed sheet blowing on a clothesline." June told him to take his time and again left the bathroom. When he finally washes with her floral scented soap, dries himself, and returns to the bedroom wearing a thick white towel, he finds her resting against the pillows, her legs stretched out in front of her. She is listening to some moody, soft music. At the sight of him, she springs up and coaxes him on to the bed for the promised massage.

Her hands are gentle and yet firm. As she kneads his shoulder muscles, June explains that massage is one of the courses that she has taken at the Institute. It seems an unlikely subject for a singer, but Bran is too relaxed to think about anything but the almost sensual caresses of June's fingers. She works for a while on his spine, and he begins to feel aroused as she plays him like an instrument.

"Feeling better?"

"That was great. Thanks." She turns her eyes on him, a look that is both solemn and resolute. She gets up and goes into the bathroom. Bran turns over and sinks into the bed, grateful for his turn of good fortune. He is safe and comfortable, the sheets smell of lavender and are smooth against his skin, and the bed is firm yet soft. He is curious about June. He wants to know something about her and about this school or whatever it is. All of this is revolving in his head when she returns wearing a thin, cotton nightgown cut low at the bodice and she slides into the bed next to him without a word.

He lies back on the soft pillow breathing the scent of lavender and June reaches up and turns off the electric light next to the bed leaving the room in ambivalent darkness, daubed with the milky phosphorescence of moonlight. June lies on her back, her head pressed into the center of her soft pillow.

"I'd like to tell you something about myself, if you care to hear it."

"Yes," he quickly answers, and at once she starts to speak, her voice gentle, unemotional, almost the tone of a mother telling a bed- time story to her young child. She had been brought to the Institute ten years before, against her will. She was abducted as she walked home from school.

Bran listens horrified as June continues in the same reflective tone as if she were talking about a make-believe world. June moves her head closer to him and he feels her soft hair brush his cheek and smells the herbal scent of her shampoo. The fragrance and touch arouses him again but he recoils, embarrassed and confused by his reaction. June lies back and continues. Once the children had resigned themselves to their fate, life was comfortable, even good. They are well educated, well fed, have good clothes, books, culture, so that in time they might mix with the highest social strata and hold their own in conversation and manners.

"What about the ones who fight back?"

"Not worth it," she says with emotion, and she explains that those who fight back are threatened with an overdose of a drug that reduces the intelligence to the level of a compliant moron. These are sold as gardener's assistants and dishwashers. The smart children neither resist nor try to escape. The risks are simply too great and besides the drugs take away most of the spirit of rebelliousness.

Institute graduates are prepared for three principal vocations; professional athletics, entertainment, and companionship of both sexes. The latter ranges from the well-rounded companion to the rich and famous, to prostitution. Every student is indentured for five years after graduation, working for luxurious accommodation but little more. Then they are free to continue in the same field, paying a modest share of their earnings to the Institute, or to pursue another livelihood of their choosing.

By the time June has finished, Bran is wide awake. His first impulse is to leave this very night, but he checks it. Instead, a few questions come to mind. "Who runs this place?" he asks, thinking that they must be outlaws of the lowest grade, those who make a living through murder and violence.

June's answer is as surprising as everything else he has learned that night. "It's a kind of church: the Temple of Hermaphrodite." The mythological figure, Hermaphrodite, became both man and woman when a female nymph who loved him merged her body with his. The cult believes that the highest form of human life carries the best characteristics of male and female. "The ideal person has a warrior's courage combined with a mother's compassion, the physical form of a young boy, ripened by a young woman's breasts, hips, buttocks, hair, and fine facial features. Facial hair and body hair, for example, is akin to the lower primates and to be spurned."

In contrast to the manner in which she recounted her abduction, Bran sees that June is enthusiastic as she describes the ideal human.

"Do you agree with all that?"

"Oh yes." Her head nods a few times as she says this. "You have to admit that we are beautiful; you've said as much. And though there are differences among us, the best of us are noble, honorable, great companions, loyal to the end, and responsive to the needs of our friends, even to our own detriment. That's what we are taught."

"Well, I..."

Radiating a confidential, seductive charm, her dusty voice sincere and convincing, she says, "Believe me, Bran, if you had me as a friend and companion you would have no need of another. I would be everything to you."

June turns toward him, and he can feel her intensity as, out of nowhere, she asks, "Bran, can I trust you?"

"Everybody else does," he replies, smiling at her serious tone.

"I'm not joking." she says with a mild reproof. Without waiting for a response, she continues and her complex mellifluous voice is so seductive and compelling that he would have found it hard to say no to her. She turns on the light looks at him soberly. "I want to leave. Will you help me?"

"Why, after all these years, do you want to leave now?"

"They want to indenture me as early as next month. I met the man who would be my master for five years. He is a wealthy Iranian. Lives in Teheran. Wants me to teach his children to be cultured. And he wants me for his sex slave. That's my future." Resolve hardens her gaze. "Will you help me get away?" she asks, her eyes boring into him.

To put off answering, he asks a question. "Who is this Dr...?"

She props her head up on one elbow and tells him about Dr. Shiksal, the Superintendent of the Institute, an ostensibly mild-mannered geneticist and classical scholar who has little regard for the wishes, or for that matter, the lives of his charges, in his pursuit of perfection of the human form. There is a fondness in her voice that horrifies Bran for he can't understand how anyone could respect someone who has abducted them. When she has finished, he says as much and June looks at him with an increasingly evident sweet-sadness.

"Will you help me leave?" she repeats.

Bran looks across the room at his pack and thinks about the importance of his mission. Reluctantly he says, "It depends on what you want me to do, June."

She explains that all she needs is someone to travel with, at least as far as Fresno. She will get out on her own. He rests his head on the pillow and wonders how much more complicated his mission might get. At the rate he is picking people up, he will arrive in Los Angeles with a full hyde ball team. If it is no more than that, she would be welcome.

"Let's get some sleep. If it's anything like today, tomorrow will be a long one."

Her eyes glow and she says with an open grin, "Then you'll help."

"How could I refuse you?" he replies hoping he won't regret it.

THE THIRD DAY

—1—

June is already up and dressed in worn jeans and work-shirt when Bran awakes, instantly alert. A small blue knapsack is full of what he assumes is June's clothing. Her hair is tied loosely behind her head and a thick wave is brushing her broad cheek.

"Won't that pack give you away?"

"No, everyone has one." She looks cheerful and excited as she urges him to hurry or they will miss breakfast.

As they walk the gravel paths in the pale morning sun Bran looks around with new eyes. A few students wander together laughing and nodding about something. Someone, a boy, or is it a girl, passes them with an absorbed expression, a book pressed against the chest. Three runners jog past in dark blue shorts and singlets, and a gardener is scraping the dark ground around a shrub with a long-handled hoe. All so ordered, so stable, and yet under it all an invisible structure that seems to him to be diabolical.

June explains calmly that he and the others should leave by the main gate, walk, or if they are lucky, ride to the junction of the highway, and she will meet him there.

"You can't just walk out with us?"

"No. We can only leave in groups and with one of the supervisors. But never mind, I've been planning this for six months," and she tells him that, although the wall around the compound is electrified, there is an old padlocked door in the wall, screened by shrubbery, for which she has a "sort of key." She gives him her pack, asking him to carry it to the rendezvous, where the road to the Institute meets the highway. "That way they won't even suspect me." It sounds simple enough to Bran.

Jonah and Nikanor are just finishing a breakfast of hot cereal, fresh wheat bread, and herb tea when Bran and June arrive. "Well, Bran, you missed the performance last night. Several of the musicians spied Nikanor's violin case and roped him into playing. I performed a few simple tricks, sleight of hand, as well," says Jonah, looking self-satisfied and communicating with a leer the assumption that Bran has spent the night with June. "Have you seen Ephus?" Bran asks looking at each of them. Neither has seen him although both, having slept in a room at the end of the stable, were up early owing to a horse that had taken to kicking the wall.

"They must have taken him," says June in a barely audible whisper. "That little event that we saw last night was probably an examination of sorts."

Bran feels his spine contract. He clenches his fists and leans forward ready to charge into the office of doctor, what- ever his name is, and pull him out of his chair. Then he thinks about his mission and, swallowing to repress his anger, he says in a low but strident voice, "How could they?"

Her only answer is a weary stare.

"What if I go to the head of this place and tell them he's my brother. Won't they let him go?"

"They won't admit they have him and you won't be able to search the place. If you persist, you'll just get a clout on the head and be tossed out the front gate; that is if you're lucky." Bran shakes his head in disbelief.

Both Nikanor and Jonah are leaning close trying to hear the conversation. Looking as if nothing has happened, June casually slathers some apricot jam on a slice of bread, stands up and says, in no more than a whisper, "We're attracting attention. Finish your breakfast and meet me behind the stable in about ten minutes." She turns an innocent smile toward Nikanor and walks at a languid pace toward the door that leads to the kitchen, even stopping to chat with one of the busboys as if she has nothing on her mind and no place to go.

Muttering to Nikanor that there is a problem he needs help with, Bran eats without appetite, for the dread has turned his insides to lead. In a few words he tells Nikanor and Jonah what has probably happened and starts to formulate a plan of rescue. June must know where they are keeping Ephus, he assumes. He will convince Nikanor and June to help free him. Yet guilt and frustration blurs his resolution for he knows that he must stop short of putting his mission at risk even if it means abandoning Ephus to June's fate.

They leave the dining room and Bran notes Nikanor's casual, yet deliberate, observation of his surroundings. In contrast Ephus's abduction has turned Jonah peevish and he urges them to leave with or without the waif, "who has probably just run off like a half-wild stray." As they walk toward the stable Bran tells them what he hopes to do to rescue Ephus.

Nonplused as if he'd been told when the bus would arrive, Nikanor says only, "You think this girl can help get him out of here?"

Rounding the corner of the stable they see June leaning against an old live oak, mending a bridle. She looks up barely acknowledging them and goes back to the stitching with a sharp leather awl. All three sit down near her and she comes right to the point in a soft voice, "The boy has to be in the receiving building."

"Can we get him out?" asks Bran.

"What's this we?" says Jonah.

"I can tell you how to do it but it's risky. There are two attendants, big specimens. They are strong and skilled in the martial arts. There's only one door to the place and the first attendant is outside. I walked by just now."

"How about a window?"

"Barred. There's no way to get in without dealing with the attendants. And with your bad shoulder there's nothing you could do without a gun."

"One of us could distract him and another come up behind and hit him on the head." Bran looks at the others, trying to gauge their willingness to help.

"Well count me out, Bran," says Jonah. "I'm not strong and I have a weak heart. Besides I can't make good time with these cans."

"To hell with the cans. They're Ephus's cans anyhow."

With a pallid and apologetic expression barely covering his fear, Jonah whines, "You're fifteen years too late for my help. I'll wait for you at the crossroad." With that he picks up his pack and the cans and slouches toward the main gate.

Bran turns to June, "How about you?"

Torment twists her features; she drops the hand holding the bridle and says, "What you're asking could finish my escape plans."

"It might be a way to put those principles of yours to a test," Bran says, staring into her eyes with challenge.

June's own eyes narrow with reproach and Bran can see the indecision as she draws her lips together. She gets up and walks a few steps away from them, turns suddenly and says, "Wait here," She goes into the stable and returns with two coils of rope which she throws to Nikanor.

He looks at Bran with an open grin. "I guess that means I'm coming too."

"I never doubted it," says Bran.

"I'll have to deal with both of the attendants." June's steady gaze takes them both in with the look of the person in charge. "Both of you stay out of sight but be prepared to help if I get in trouble and to truss up the first one if I succeed."

Incredulous, Bran says, "Are you strong enough to get the better of him?"

"You asked for my help, now take it as it comes." June bites down on her full lower lip and says in a softer tone, "I know where he's vulnerable." She walks on and they follow at a distance of five paces. The building is a small barracks in an isolated part of the compound. Shrubs line the paths, and the entrance is flanked by two ancient cedar trees, their long branches touching. A flutter of June's hand, and they move out of sight keeping a view of the building through the screen of bushes.

A man with the physique of a wrestler gone soft in middle age is slouched on a bench beside the door reading a newspaper. At sight of June, he slowly stands and greets her with a smile. She gets very close to him, moving her body and head with animation as she talks for what seems to Bran to be five minutes, and he must restrain himself from rushing at the man. What, after all, could this slender person do to this bear?

Almost afraid to breathe, Bran watches as the man relaxes, laughs and shakes his head to the side. The motion of his head has reached its limit and his glance is fixed for just an instant on the trees when June's right foot flies up to his groin. He groans and bends over as her arm and fingertips thrust like a dagger into his Adam's apple. With a strangled gasp he lurches toward her, but she sidesteps and, using the back of her right hand like an axe, she chops the back of his neck. He falls like a tree. Nikanor drags the unconscious man into the bushes and binds and gags him while June searches his pockets for his keys.

"I'm glad she's on our team," says Nikanor as June walks to the door of the building, and lets herself in.

A minute later a thin forearm in a blue work shirt reaches out of the partially open door and a graceful hand beckons. They enter a dim corridor lit by bare light bulbs. June, panting and pale, is standing over a huge man sprawled on the floor face down, unconscious.

"How did you manage that?" Nikanor asks staring with admiration.

"With pleasure; this one is a first-rate bastard. Tie him and we'll lock him in a room. Bran, your colt is in room eight." June goes into a room and returns with the keys but Bran has already rushed down the hall.

They find Ephus asleep on a cot. "Drugged," says June as they get him on his feet. Bran shakes him awake and is relieved when the boy recognizes him through half-closed eyes. Holding him up between them, they drag him down the hall. Again, June goes into the room, she opens a medicine cabinet and pulls one of the small bottles off the shelf. She produces a pill and forces it down Ephus's throat. "We must leave by the shrubs. There's a little path against the outer wall and my little fairy door is just a hundred yards from here."

They leave the building, she locks the door, throws the keys into the bushes and they fight through the dense screen of privet and English laurel into a narrow passage against the high outer wall. Branches lashing at them, they eventually come to a low, padlocked door of thick wooden boards faded to silver by age and exposure.

"My key," June says, displaying a notched piece of brass, which she inserts into the lock. After working the makeshift key, she turns to them looking concerned. "I can't open it! It seems to be frozen." Nikanor patiently takes the improvised key and tries but eventually he gives up as well.

"Only one thing to do," says Bran. He takes two steps back against the bending shrubs and lunges at the boards of the door with his good shoulder. Although it rattles, the rusty screws of the lock hasp hold fast. On the third try the wood splinters, and the door opens, throwing him forward on to the ground outside the wall.

June rushes out behind him and she extends her arms as if to grasp and embrace the sky. As they walk away from the wall into the undergrowth, Nikanor says, "I think you can handle yourself, June. But you'll probably find soon enough that being outside that wall is harder than being locked up in a canary cage."

"I'm ready for whatever comes my way."

"Move faster," says Bran in the lead.

—2—

Gunther Shiksal , PhD., Director of the Institute, is seated behind the Queen Anne style mahogany table that serves as his desk. His office on the third floor of the administration building is tastefully appointed and fastidiously neat with papers and books each in their proper place. The brown walls are decorated with framed etchings of classical statuary from the Greek and Roman times; athletes, heroes, gods, and demi-gods, all perfectly proportioned. A slight, mild looking man with thin grey hair pasted back in stripes and dominating baleful brown eyes set in pouches, Shiksal has the unique educational background of animal genetics and classical Greek history, a perfect combination for a man who is the moving force behind the Hermaphrodite Temple and its Institute for Self-Realization.

The disturbing news of the discovery of two security guards bound and gagged, the disappearance of the boy taken in for observation, and most important the identification of June, one of his favorite students, as the perpetrator, has activated his chronic indigestion. Looking across the table at his assistant, Carlos Fuerta, he reaches for his antacid pills, kept at hand in a little Limoges sugar bowl, and coughs.

He swallows the pills and, dropping his eyelids, says in a voice soft as gentle wind, "What a pass. Such events always have an effect on the morale of the students. We shall have to tell them that June was killed defending the property of the Institute against outlaws who grossly abused our hospitality. A memorial service will be scheduled for tomorrow morning with chorus and a brazier to be kindled to burn for twenty-four hours."

"That should work very nicely," says Carlos, making a note in a small notebook that he always carried with him. He is a dark man, slender and well proportioned, who was a flamenco dancer before injuring his leg in a fall when a trap door suddenly opened under him during a performance. "And that leaves June," he says looking at the Director. Shiksal frowns and spins toward the window in his English walnut swivel chair. He stares down at a soccer game in progress on the athletic field and ponders. He doesn't want to take June's life. It is such a waste of those years of shaping her physically, spiritually, and intellectually. To destroy her would be like shooting a thoroughbred horse because it has kicked a groom to death. And yet there are the rules to be followed, principles to be adhered to, for what is a life if principles once arrived at are not followed. He rotates back toward Carlos and says with a weary look, "Give truth to the lie, Carlos. June will no doubt go to Fresno with her new companions. Tell our friends at the Labor Contractors Association to find her and dispose of her lovely body as they do."

"It's a terrible waste. Couldn't we make an exception?" Carlos leans forward in earnest. "After all, the school won't know the difference."

His gaze both weary and stern, Shiksal says without hesitation, "I will know the difference. That's more important." But another twinge of irresolution nags at his stomach and he reaches again for the antacid bowl.

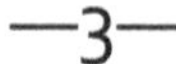

Bran and his companions soon find a trail through the scrub that seems to follow the road toward the main highway, and they move along at a fast walk hoping to reach the road before someone at the Institute discovers what they have done. The stimulant that June has given Ephus has done its job and he is almost back to normal. Bran is eager to find out what has happened to him, but they talk only when necessary. He walks along behind the others listening for the sounds of pursuers, thinking about the day's events, as strange and dangerous as the day before, and he wonders with foreboding if the whole trip will be this tough. His hopeful attitude steps in and he tells himself that once they get to Fresno the worst will be over. Even though he now has so many companions, each of whom seem to complicate and delay his journey, it is equally true that they have all been helpful in their way. Jonah has straightened out his shoulder, Ephus has helped, and June has saved Ephus. As for Nikanor, just having that tall even-tempered man along makes him feel supported.

The path ultimately takes them right to the intersection of the road, and as they break through the screen of Manzanita, they find Jonah sitting on the pack of flattened cans, cleaning his fingernails with a little knife. He starts with alarm as they break into the open, then as he recognizes them his expression changes to one of exaggerated welcome and he slaps Bran on the shoulder as though he'd known him for years. "I knew you'd manage to find the boy without me. Besides, how could I have kept up with this burden? I hope it doesn't prove to be a waste of my energy."

Ephus says with a challenge, "I found them cans and don't you ferget it."

"You can be sure I won't."

At Bran's urging they cross the highway and sit down, screened from both roads by the cover of small trees and brush. Bran passes around a little bread, cheese, and sausage from his pack, and they discuss the safest way to get to Fresno.

"The next town down the road is Somer Springs, beyond the Inspection Station. You can get a bus from there, right to Fresno," says Nikanor.

Jonah has seen a car from the Institute heading toward the check point. They conclude that the safest way is to avoid the inspection. With Nikanor and Ephus in front and Bran bringing up the rear, they move away from the highway and find a well-trod path. Despite the danger Bran is enjoying the hike; it is one of the things he loves to do, and walking is preferable to the stifling, cramped, and dangerous buses.

When they are well away from the road, June falls back and walks with Bran for a time. They walk in silence until she turns and says, with a grateful smile, "I don't know if I would have had the courage to leave if you hadn't come along."

"You're the one who deserves the thanks, for Ephus and all."

"You're fond of the boy. And I can see that he's devoted to you."

Bran felt himself flush with embarrassment. "He just reminds me of something, that's all. And he's a plucky little fox."

"Well, I want you to know that you've won yourself another friend, Bran."

"Friendship's one thing you can't get too much of," he replies. June touches him on the shoulder with a gentle hand and with her long stride she moves forward on the path leaving Bran with a spark of self-satisfaction. Gradually their path climbs through fragrant Scrub Bay toward a ridge. Still walking in the rear, Bran is the last to reach it. He joins the others, panting a little from the effort and looks down over the tops of the red bark Manzanita.

Far below them spreads the San Joaquin Valley, a vast brown blanket patched here and there with squares of green. The air is clear and, except where the wind raises packets of dust, the valley floor is sharply focused in the mature, autumn sunlight. A river sheathed in dark green meanders toward the Valley center between mottled fields. Having lived in the hills all of his life, Bran has never before seen the Great Central Valley. The scale impresses him, but his eye focuses on the little patches of cultivation. "Real sparse," he says in a subdued voice.

"The whole Valley used to be farmed," says June. "They brought water down from the mountains in great channels. They still exist but all the water goes south of Fresno now."

"Why is that?"

Nikanor looked at him and said, "The soil salted up. They used to run water through it to clean it but during the Parch there wasn't enough water for that. Normal crops won't grow in it. So, the farmers went broke and lost their land."

The image of farmers being dispossessed brought back the pain of the Glade's predicament and he said, "They just left without a fuss?"

"There was a fight. The ones around Fresno won. The ones up here didn't."

Again, Bran realized how helpful it might have been to have known what happened.

"We'd better move on if you want to get the next bus to Fresno." With that he started down the path. Bran followed wondering why Nikanor was so familiar with the trails.

Split by the road out of the mountains, the village squats at the base of the slope; a warren of tin-roofed, weathered, wooden houses surrounding the cavity of an unpaved market.

They stop at the outskirts and look down the street at three children dressed in faded clothing chasing each other with sticks.

Nikanor turns to June and says, "You'd be safer if you could get right on the bus and try to look invisible till it leaves. Your friends from the Institute might have figured by now that you made it this far. You'll find the bus, a blue and yellow one, parked on the other side of the market in a lot." He looks at his watch. "You haven't got a lot of time."

"Aren't you coming with us?" asks Bran, aware that he's come to rely on Nikanor's support.

Nikanor looks at him with affection and regret. "I've got an errand. But I might see you in Fresno." He gives them directions to a hostel where June might be reasonably safe. With that they shake hands, clasp shoulders, and June reaches up and kisses Nikanor on the cheek. What business does a wandering fiddle player have in a fly-blown place like this? Bran wonders, before his attention shifts to the sight of the market around the bend of the street.

—4—

The market consists of tight rows of improvised tables or ground cloths piled with anything the vendor believes people might need; tomatoes, nuts and bolts, potatoes, underwear, cucumbers, or used eyeglasses. Dresses hang like pennants on a line above one stall next to a pile of rag blankets across from a collage of used pots and pans, scoured pitted and mended. There is no order to the display; carcasses of skinned goats hang blood-red and fat-white next to piles of dried herbs, and the whole is bound together by a tightly milling crowd bent over wares; pinching, fondling, smelling, haggling over prices, looking both preoccupied and vacant as they search the stalls to fill their needs.

Bran, Ephus, Jonah, and June pass through the crowd as quickly as they can, moving from the smell of raw meat to the rot of vegetable. Immersed in the market's confusion they stop in front of a man, wearing all white, who is selling flour and rice out of two bins. They decide that June and Jonah would get on the bus, buy tickets, and claim seats while Ephus and Bran buy some food.

"Want me to take your pack to the bus?" asks June.

"No, I'm used to it."

"What about your shoulder? You'll have a hard time buying things."

Jonah looks from Bran to the pack and says, "He never lets that pack out of his sight, June." June agrees to loan Jonah the fare and they continue through the crowd, slower than they might, because of the cans and June's interest in everything around her. Ephus promises to make his own way to the bus and he disappears leaving Bran to elbow from one unfamiliar booth to another, buying a few tomatoes at one end, traversing the entire market to find the only bread, finally passing to the center again for a few shriveled sausages made of who knows what?

June and Jonah find the bus, just where Nikanor said it would be, parked on the edge of an unpaved, deeply rutted space shared with an assortment of bent, faded, and rusted pickup trucks and cars. They buy four tickets from the driver. Jonah waits as the driver finds a place for the cans on the roof, and June mounts the already crowded bus and finds two seats next to each other and one on the aisle for Jonah.

She sits down, crosses her arms, and looks about at the assortment of people. She breathes the stuffy air and lets her mind embrace her first day of freedom. It is a relief to have gotten on the bus without seeing the familiar green Institute car or any of the staff, and for the first time since they have escaped through the door in the wall, she feels confident that she would elude her pursuers. The impressions of the market flood her mind and she feels the excitement of freedom; the choices that suddenly are open to her to buy different things, wear different clothes, eat what she chooses, go anywhere, be anything. Even so, the awareness that she doesn't know where she will sleep tonight is a little frightening. June is so preoccupied with her thoughts that she doesn't even see Jonah take his seat across the aisle and just in front of her. But when the bus begins to vibrate she realizes that the driver is warming up the engine preparing to leave without Bran and Ephus. She gets Jonah's attention and says, "Bran hasn't gotten here yet. Shouldn't we tell the driver to wait?"

"Don't trouble yourself. They'll get here."

The engine rolls higher and falls into a throbbing idle. Sitting on the edge of her seat, June looks out the window toward the market hoping to see one or the other break out of the milling crowd.

"There's always another bus tomorrow morning," says Jonah.

"But I have their tickets." Jonah shrugs at this. As she looks anxiously through the dusty window, the bus begins to move, creeping slowly between two pick-up trucks.

"Wait!" June shouts over the whine of the gears, "There are two more passengers." The driver ignores her, and the bus continues through the narrow passage. Again, she shouts only louder and she sees the driver's frowning, narrow face in the mirror over the windshield.

He manipulates the wheel and shouts back, "Sorry, but I got a schedule to make." He pulls out of the bottleneck and begins to accelerate as June looks back and sees Bran followed by Ephus just breaking into the parking area.

"There they are!" June shouts but the driver ignores her and shifts into a higher gear moving faster toward the pavement. A rush of anger pulls June out of her seat and she lunges forward up the narrow passageway stumbling over packages. She pulls the leather awl out of the sleeve in her belt and, holding it horizontally within six inches of the driver's neck, she says, in a tone as menacing as she can make her voice, "Stop the bus and let them on or I'll put a hole in your throat with this." The driver hesitates, taking his foot off the accelerator. June's arm moves closer to his neck.

He jams on the brakes, and says, "Ok, Ok, since you could see them coming."

June's heart is pounding in her throat as she looks out the window and sees that Bran has almost caught up. Her hand trembles as she puts the awl back in the sheath and returns to her seat. Bran and Ephus clamber up the steps. He searches the crowd, sees June and the empty seat and she shifts toward the window and makes room for both of them.

"Nice of the driver to wait. He must of seen me in the mirror."

"He wasn't going to wait; not until June threatened to put a belt hole in his Adam's Apple with that leather punch of hers," says Jonah with a grim smile.

"That's the second time today I owe you thanks. You saved me a day, maybe."

June looks down, turns her eyes toward him, and says with a breathless laugh, "I told you I know how to be a friend."

—5—

The Great Valley is not as desolate as it has appeared from a distance. The unbroken stretches of dusty dry grass and baked adobe are dotted with small farms, faded frame bungalows surrounded by a few acres of vegetables behind high, barbed-wire fences. Here and there a splash of bright marigolds or yellow daisies explodes from the ground like a sign advertising a long-ago performance. Sometimes the flowers show signs of attention, fruit trees stand on parade in small groves picked clean of competing vegetation, and flimsy windmills twist idly on their makeshift wooden towers, leaching water from the ground. But between the patches of vegetation only the wind tends the wild clump grass. Vacant houses with black holes where windows and doors have been, partially collapsed barns, fenceposts, grey as driftwood, recall a better time. Bran stares at the abused valley and is seized by its desolation.

"Bran," says Jonah, "what do you think we'll get for these cans?

"I never sold any cans before."

"You never did say what you're going to Fresno for," says Jonah, turning an appraiser's eye on Bran's pack, crammed under his legs.

"Some cows we've got to sell," replies Bran wishing Jonah would fall asleep.

"Have you got a coin?" Jonah persists, and Bran fishes into his pocket and hands him a quarter. He watches as Jonah rolls the coin across his knuckles. The man next to Jonah, a farmer in worn jeans and a tan work shirt, grey stubble of beard on his long wrinkled face, looks on as the coin appears and disappears. Seeing the man's interest, Jonah makes the coin appear out of the farmer's ear.

Dusk liquefies the landscape; burnt orange from the setting sun fills the western sky over the far range of hills, while blue-grey clouds, thin as eels, take on body and darken. In a field not far from the road, Bran sees two groups of men, dressed in tightly fitting black clothes, fighting with knives and chains. Two of them lay on the ground writhing and holding their sides, two others are rolling over one another. The rest dance about, semi- crouched, knives extended at the waist, lunging, darting back and taunting. It reminds him of a fight he'd once witnessed between two stags. June is watching as well.

"I've heard of that. It's a game that they play until one side gives up," she says, her face drawn and sober.

"Why?"

"They must enjoy it."

"How could anybody enjoy intentionally hurting somebody?"

June looks at him thoughtfully. "It might feel satisfying; righting a wrong or taking revenge."

Bran recalls the time Peter, Mavis's brother, hit him on the back of the head with a flung stone; he still has the scar. They had been no more than eight. He remembers Peter's look of malicious triumph. It had given Bran no satisfaction that he had attacked Peter and bloodied his nose. Both children had been told by Leah that to injure another, without good cause, is a profanation of life.

"Anybody hungry?" Jonah asks over the noise of the engine as he cuts some chunks of bread and yellow cheese that Bran has given him. He offers a piece to the man next to him who accepts it.

Ephus reaches across the aisle for a piece of cheese and asks, "Want a apple?"

"Not if it's stolen."

"Some lady give it to me. I told her I was hungry."

"If you've got some extra cheese, I'd be glad to pay for it. I didn't have time to buy something for the road," says the farmer.

"I wouldn't think of taking your money," Jonah says, handing him another chunk, but the farmer is already reaching into his back pocket for his money and looking perplexed.

"My money's gone!"

Jonah does his best to calm him. "Must of slipped out of your pocket. Stand out of your seat while I check behind you." The man lifts up and Jonah moves his hands deftly behind him. "What did I say," he says, producing a wad of money. "It was stuck in the crack of the seat."

Looking relieved the farmer counts the money as Jonah looks on nibbling on a chunk of bread. "Twenty dollars missing," the farmer says, looking sad again.

"You must of counted it wrong in the first place," says Jonah and when the farmer continues to look glum he adds, "You're pretty lucky to have found any of it. If you hadn't checked your pocket, you would have lost the whole wad." With that judgment, Jonah turns away.

Darkness slowly settles on the Valley, total darkness pierced only by a dim square of light from the kitchen of a farmhouse. With night the Valley takes on the ominous mood of the death game, and it seems to Bran that the bus is moving faster to reach the security of the city. There are no lights in the bus except for the faint yellow glow of the instrument panel and an occasional splash against the window from passing headlights. June snuggles closer to him, she puts her hand on his thigh and Bran, comforted by her touch, leaves it there. Dozing in a fitful, semi-waking state he imagines that it is Mavis beside him.

—6—

The slowing of the bus wakes Bran from a fitful doze as the narrow streets of the Free City of Fresno close around them. Inching through the foot traffic, the bus finally stops in an enclosure where several other buses are standing idle. Passengers clamber down, unload packages from the roof, and soon disperse in the company of family and friends.

Bran and his companions join the stream of people in the dark street. Jonah insists that he knows the way to the hostel of St. Procopius, but once inside the labyrinthine *Sal Si Puedes* he gives up. A child, no more than ten, shoeless, with rank blond hair, offers to take them to the hostel for 25 cents and they willingly follow him along the dark, twisting, narrow lanes. If the Institute is the consummation of order and beauty, the *Sal* is the opposite; chaotic, crowded, ugly, and foul smelling. Bran has seen poverty before but always diminished by the familiar background of ridges and trees. Here in the *Sal*, there is no relief from it.

They reach the open courtyard of a two-story adobe building. Here at least there is air to breathe, benches, a patch of grass, and even a fountain spilling from an urn into a hexagonal basin. People are seated in clusters, talking or simply stretched out among their belongings, and a group is gathered around a man playing a guitar. They are met at the door of the building by a frail looking man wearing a grey robe tied at the waist with a rope. He greets them with a warm smile, a prolonged, if weak, handshake, and looks at each of them with his gentle, black eyes in a way that makes Bran feel both noticed as a person and at ease. "Be at peace in the name of God," he says, and they pass into a wide hall, floored with worn red tiles.

To the right they see, through an open door, a high-ceilinged dining room crowded with long, dark oak tables placed end to end. At least forty people are seated in clusters eating, talking over tea, playing cards, or reading. The place is noisy, with an echo of clashing pots and eddying conversation. They approach a counter at the far end and are given a bowl of lentil soup and a chunk of still warm wheat bread. Bran takes a seat not far from the kitchen, puts his pack under his chair, and focuses on his food.

His belly filled with soup that reminds him of Leah's cooking, he sits back relaxed and content. Seduced by the protective, friendly atmosphere of the hostel, he has the feeling that the dangers of the trip are finally behind him. There is still plenty of time; another six days to get to Los Angeles by bus. He looks around. People seem road-worn but at ease. A woman at the next table, with stringy brown hair and a bad complexion, is nursing an infant. Bran catches her eye. On the far wall is a large crucifix; a tortured, suffering Christ. He had seen the same image many times in the doorway of the Catholic Church in Templeton and it had always jarred him. Now it seems to be a fitting symbol of life around the hostel.

June observes him staring at it and says, "Don't tell the priests but it gives me the chills. Why shouldn't God be beautiful rather than suffering?"

"The priests look happy enough. Maybe they think suffering is beautiful."

June rolls her tongue around the front of her teeth, shifts her head thoughtfully. "Are you leaving tomorrow?"

"At dawn. I want to be sure I get a bus south."

"Mind if I come with you?" There is hope and a vulnerable plea in her eyes as she says this and any resistance he might have to traveling further with anyone other than Ephus evaporates.

"I can't stop you," he replies with a wide smile, acknowledging that he would be glad of the company.

"It's better if I keep moving. They'll be looking for me here."

Jonah listens and watches them with his shrewd crow's eyes. He puts his spoon down and, reverting to his theatrical formalism, says, "Then alas we part, friends. Life's highway has many crossroads, so to speak." They turn their heads simultaneously and stare as they might look at an oddity and Jonah mutters, "It's been nice." He goes back to the counter for a second helping. Bran slings his pack over his good shoulder and follows.

"I'll watch it for you," says June but Bran pretends not to hear her.

"What have you got in that pack, Bran?" asks Jonah gazing at him with an analytical squint.

"The last of that good sausage."

He has just returned to his place when he sees Nikanor following a stout priest into the room. Nikanor and the priest go to the counter for some food and join Bran and the others at the table. Father Malachi, the Priest, is a cheerful looking man with a frog's double chin and pouchy cheeks who, Nikanor explains, runs the hostel.

"How did you get here so fast?" Bran asks.

"A friend gave me a ride," Nikanor's eyes keep drifting to the door as if he is expecting someone. After no more than ten minutes a slight man, wearing a brown beret pulled low on his forehead and a worn leather motorcycle jacket, appears at the door and looks around with a worried expression. Bran sees Nikanor's pale eyes make contact with him, and the man weaves his way among the tables and hands Nikanor a piece of paper. He looks at it, stands up, and takes a few steps down the aisle. The man follows and they talk.

Nikanor is returning to his seat when five men in blue uniforms and carrying machine pistols burst into the room and fan out. "Police inspection!" one shouts. "Stay where you are and keep calm. Please have your documents ready."

Bran looks to Nikanor for guidance, but his face is an emotionless mask as he sits down, glances at Father Malachi, and hunches over his tea looking a foot smaller. The priest gets up and walks toward the police saying in a resolute voice, "This is a sanctuary. You know that you have no right to come in here without a court order." The policeman stares at him. Without responding he motions to his men and they move toward the nearest tables. With a scrape of a chair the man in the beret starts toward the kitchen.

Seeing him, a policeman raises his gun and shouts "Stop!"

Instead, the man throws himself across a table, lands on the other side and runs toward the door. The clatter of the machine pistol tears through the room. Bran watches, frozen with horror as the man leaps up, arms outstretched grasping the air. His head jerks back spasmodically, a spray of blood and flesh fan out of him as a horizontal row of bullets stitch his back and he slowly collapses to the floor. Screams and shouts erupt and people drop to the floor seeking cover. Father Malachi rushes toward the fallen man as two policemen shove their way between the tables, staring briefly at people, prodding the ones on the floor with the muzzles of their guns. Another policeman runs around the edge of the room toward the kitchen.

Bran looks down the aisle and sees Nikanor crawling on his hands and knees between the jumble of overturned chairs. As Bran watches hoping that Nikanor can make it to the kitchen, another policeman rushes down an aisle to a point just across the table from Bran, raises his gun and takes aim at Nikanor's back. Bran wheels out of his seat, lifts the table, and turns it over on the policeman at the moment the gun goes off. Bullets wildly spray the wall nearly cutting the crucifix in two. As the officer struggles to regain his balance, Bran lunges across the overturned table and chops the side of the policeman's head with the edge of his good hand. The man staggers back against the next table.

Get out of here, Bran tells himself and he rushes laterally down the aisle toward the kitchen but he stumbles over a chair and falls to the floor. He is up on his knees when his head explodes, a diamond shatters and dissolves to black.

—7—

Nikanor hears the shots and knows they are meant for him. He rushes toward the kitchen on his hands and knees. He steals a glance over his shoulder just as Bran strikes the policeman. If only someone would put out the lights. He has to take the chance that he can get to the door of the kitchen without being hit. Looking under the table he sees legs wearing dark blue running toward the same door.

He grabs a chair and lunges for the kitchen door on a collision course with the policeman. Just then the lights go out. The surprised look on the square face of the policeman remains in Nikanor's mind as an after-mage as he swings the chair like a bat and feels it crackle against the man's chest. Nikanor wheels, he drops the chair and runs toward the kitchen as bullets whistle and spatter the wall. Momentarily stunned, he bounces against the wall, gropes to the left, finds the door and pushes through into the kitchen.

The kitchen is familiar to him and he rushes to the large commercial refrigerator, hoping that the police are still stumbling around in the dining room. The cook and a priest have already moved it out just enough for him to slip through and into a hatch in the wall no more than three feet wide. It is not the first time he has done this, and he grips the hemp rope and quickly lets himself down to the basement. He gropes around for the flashlight that hangs on a hook, listening as the refrigerator is moved back against the wall. Nikanor lights the flashlight and runs to the other side of the building to a small room; he opens the door of an old wardrobe, slips aside a wooden panel and crawls through. The cone of light from his flashlight probes the low, barely four-foot-high walls of a tunnel supported with posts and lintels of rough sawn wood. He replaces the wooden panel and looks at an old Smith and Wesson 38 in a leather pouch hanging next to the opening. Guns trouble him--there is always the temptation to use them-- and he hesitates before taking the weapon. Nikanor removes it from its pouch and puts it into his pocket feeling the cold steel rub uncomfortably against his leg. He turns and rests, waiting for his heartbeat and breathing to slow. A headache is already beginning to throb, but he ignores it. He is safe. After a minute or so he begins to trot as fast as he can in a crouch. The rank air smells of rat droppings, reminding him of the basements of apartment houses in Detroit. The beam of the flashlight dances from the walls to the ceiling and as he goes on, he inspects the condition of the joints, pleased that there is no sign of damp rot.

A civil engineer by profession, Nikanor had supervised the construction of the tunnels, mindful of the hiding places of the early Christians in the Roman catacombs. In all there was a mile and a half of them. They are used not just for communication but as a storage depot for scarce goods that could be sold to raise money, spare parts, hospital supplies and enough weapons for a small revolution. Although Unity America is officially committed in its Constitution to the restoration of the pre-Dissolution democracy by non-violent means, one faction of the ruling body believed that the arms would be needed very soon.

Nikanor relaxes enough to go more slowly. His back is beginning to cramp from bending over. He has plenty of time for he won't surface until he is sure the police have left the *Sal*. After no more than fifteen minutes in the tunnel he comes to the ladder that will take him to the basement of the best silversmith in the *Sal*, Ben Firman, known as Paul. Everyone has another name and Nikanor has no less than five. He slips down, leans his back against the cool earth, and breathes deeply. That made 23 escapes since the siege of Detroit, sixteen years ago, he recalls with weary satisfaction. The "Cat" is in fact one of his names, but he has long ago exceeded his nine lives. It is nothing short of a miracle that he has so far escaped with not more than a few minor injuries; a bullet in his thigh and a knife wound that grazed a rib.

There was a time when he had taken pleasure in outwitting the police. Now it is just a matter of survival. Not even his own survival; that had long ago ceased to matter—his life burned in Detroit—the survival of his work is all that matters now. And even that gives him little pleasure, if satisfaction could be separated from pleasure. He no longer enjoys the constant travel but still can't give it up for he alone knits the cellular organization together. For security sake, except for the staff at the Center, no unit has more than twelve members, no unit leader knows more than six others and only the Counsel of Ten know Nikanor's true function. Wherever he goes he is known to members by one name or another, one role or another. For the most part he is regarded either as a middle-line organizer or a courier and assessment collector named Nikanor. Some see him as a man who knows just where to place the plastic explosive to topple an electric tower using so little plastic that it fits into the false bottom of his battered violin case. He has survived and traveled as freely as he does largely because of the incompetence and corruption of the police. One in three accept bribes knowing them to come from Unity America, particularly in Fresno where just about every business pays assessments to UA. Every business but the biggest, Standard, the largest landowner in the valley, the only one which had successfully managed to deal with the nitrate and salt pollution that had poisoned the soil. Even Standard pays their taxes one way or another.

Nikanor thinks of the refinery at San Pedro, California's principal port of entry for foreign crude oil. If the operation comes off as planned, the refinery will be crippled for months. He closes his eyes and imagines the catalytic cracker exploding with a great pillar of fire, like the one that had guided the Israelites.

This too would be a beacon. The planning meetings would conclude this week and soon he will be in Los Angeles working out the details with the team. He shifts position and thinks back on his first days in California. It continually amazed him that he had started with only six contacts. Now it is getting close to the time when he would give it up. Someone else could take his job. He is just too old, too tired to play hide and seek much longer. But who else could do what he did? He goes through a dozen names of his colleagues and finds fault with each one of them.

His mind drifts to Bran and he wonders whether he has survived the attack on the policeman. Nikanor is compassionate but the endless secretive years have made him suppress his feeling for others. Too many friends, family, loved ones, are gone; too many people he had grown to trust, to rely on, are dead. Rather than suffer the loss it is better to deal on the surface with all of them; his work in fact requires it. He must get what he can out of everyone for the good of Unity America and move on like those birds he had read about in college that spend their whole life on the wing. Fatigue is weighing him down. It must be the lack of oxygen. He would like to sleep but he can't do that for here in this quiet place he might not wake for hours, and he would miss his meeting. There is always another meeting. Meetings are spun together like a web.

Bran comes back to him again, Bran and the curious June; his companions on the road, two of hundreds. Human beings held so many surprises. Hope always renewed itself. A dog could have expectation, waiting at a table for some morsels. Only the human species is capable of hope, and humanity is its only source; the blessing and the curse of the world, a preacher had called it. Nikanor switches on the flashlight and looks at his watch. Soon it will be time to go up. A mole must be a contented animal much of the time, alone in its hole without enemies. He whimsically turns the flashlight on the ceiling and looks for roots. But of course, there would be no roots since the *Sal* has few trees. Time to leave the underworld. What is the name of the Greek god? He has never been strong on remembering names. He stands and looks back down the dark tunnel imagining for a moment that his wife would appear and follow him. The dead don't come back but they don't leave you either, he thinks, and the image of his wife vanishes as he grips the rope that will bring him to the surface.

—8—

Spine wrenching chill and a nauseating throbbing ache in his head. Something hard and cold pressing against Bran becomes a damp concrete surface on which he lays stomach down. He tries to open his eyes, but a white searchlight drives bullets of pain into his head. Again, he opens his eyes and the smooth, grey surface of the floor comes into focus. He extends his vision down the floor and sees the square legs of a table and the dark legs of two or three people. Images trickle through a sieve into his consciousness and Bran remembers overturning a table and trying to get away.

He is pulled to his feet and dropped onto a straight-backed wooden chair. He closes his eyes to escape the harsh glare of the light but as he grows more aware he hears a buzzing whisper through the ringing in his ears. Fog wraps him and he is falling until the smell of something strong burns his nostrils. From across a void a hollow voice comes to him speaking words that at first, he can't understand. Then the words take shape in his head, although they have no meaning to him until he realizes that he is in the hands of the police.

"What is your role in Unity America?" asks the voice, detached, yet insistent and determined. The voice presses him with variations of the same question but he disclaims any knowledge.

Then another voice, almost friendly, asks, "Tell us all you know about Nikanor."

He tells the truth, but it seems that they can't accept that he would risk his own life to save a mere acquaintance. The questions go on; monotonous, dispassionate, the questioner at times sounding almost indifferent. They leave off talking about Nikanor and another person, his voice harsh and raw with an underlying menace, asks him where he came from and what he is doing in Fresno. Bran lies, knowing that he has no documents to refute his story. The man asks for details, going over and over the same things, trying to catch him in an inconsistency. Someone hands him a cup of hot herbal tea, and he takes it with a trembling hand, but something tells him not to drink it. Finally, one of the men enters the ring of light, and Bran recoils at the sight, for the questioner is wearing a hood that covers his entire head with just two narrow openings for his eyes and nostrils.

"We know that you are lying about everything," the man says. "Nikanor has been caught and he has implicated you already." The words jolt him as though he has been hit by a rock. Afraid but still calm, Bran knows it to be a lie, a feint to throw him off. He looks up and realizes that the man is measuring his reaction.

He shakes his head and says, "I've never even heard of Unity. If he says that, he's lying." The man gazes at him and he sees through the hole in the hood part of an emotionless blue eye staring out of what might have been a void. The interrogator turns and walks out of the light. The questions stop. There is a silence, and then he hears a clicking that he recognizes as the push buttons of a phone. The more pleasant of the voices begins speaking, not to him but to someone on the phone, very likely his wife for he is asking with solicitude about a sick person.

"Does she still have a fever?" pause "What is it?" pause "It's too late for the drug store. Just give her a kiss for me." The receiver clicks and the same voice begins again, not unpleasantly, as if the memory of his concern for the child is still weighing on him. "You have assaulted a policeman, seriously injured him. He could die. What you say to us could get you a light sentence, even get you off entirely."

"I don't know any more than I've told you," he says, hoping that this man, who could show feeling for a sick child, would believe him.

"Listen carefully," the man says in a deliberate cadence. "People sometimes get hurt in this jail. They fall down stairs or hit their heads on sharp corners. Sometimes the injuries are permanent." He paused. "Give some thought to what I've said. There's a clock on the wall behind you. When the second hand goes around once, we expect you to tell us everything, for your possible freedom."

Bran hears a chair scrape. He can see the clock in his mind, the second hand sweeping the dial, and he feels fear rising out of his gut, freezing in his chest. What could he say to them? And what would they do? He could make something up, but it would just get him in more trouble. Then they would be sure that he is lying and hold him as an accomplice. Maybe they are bluffing. He grasps at hope. The truth is all he can give them.

"Tell us what you know," the voice says calmly.

"Only what I've told you."

Two guards force him to his feet, tear his pants open and pull them down to his knees. One of them attaches metal clamps to his scrotum and an agonizing shock rip through his mid-section as though he is being bored through with a high-speed drill. He smells his own flesh burning and is about to pass out when the pain stops; but not for long. Again, he denies knowledge, and a second shock strikes him like a fist in the groin. He doubles up and groans, feeling as though he is being perforated by hundreds of needles. When the shock stops, his groin muscles are locked in a painful spasm. They question him again, repeat the torture until gradually, he seems to float away from himself, aware that below him his body is suffering, but for some reason he is free of it.

—9—

It seems to Mavis that Leah never leaves the kitchen of the Glade. She has become the soul of cooking; her very sweat smells of onions, frying fat, and raw turnips. Leah is sitting with her ham-like forearm planted like a tapering pillar on the table, cupping the sagging flesh of her face. Her kindly, perpetually red-rimmed, pale blue eyes shift from one to the other of her children.

Mavis rubs the back of her head and decides to put the worry out of her mind. There is nothing to be done but to wait and hope for the best. She looks at her mother and tries to put on a tranquil face. How fat mom has grown. It's as if she absorbs nutrients from the odors of stews and soups so thick a spoon would stand up in them. It wasn't that she ate that much, but she is always tasting. Mavis recalls how she was ten years ago: erect, her proportions larger than life, the strong well-shaped features of a half-finished carving. No one worked harder than Leah and she couldn't be persuaded to stop.

"It's what I like to do," Leah always said. It is as if she, Peter, and Bran had been raised in the kitchen among the aluminum pots; a few so big that a child could hide in them. You always knew where to find her but she always left off from whatever she was doing and paid attention to a child's needs.

"Mice got'ta eat too, don't they ma?" says Peter.

Leah shakes her head, and the double chin follows, a little slower than the rest of her face. "Not in my kitchen."

Mavis looks across the table at Peter. Like Mavis and Bran, he loves these quiet moments after the kitchen help have finished cleaning up and gone back to their cabins for the night. They would sit in the warm circle of light from a single lamp around the sanded, ashen surface of the table, drinking mint tea, eating left-over cake, talking over the little happenings that distinguished one day from the other. It was best in the winter with a wind howling around the corners of the kitchen, rattling the window frames, while they sat with their shoes off eating apple turnovers or left-over bread with this year's plum jam. Mavis looks at the fourth side of the table and she is overcome with a sense of danger. She tries to ignore it by concentrating on Peter, with his square face and broad bridged nose.

"Bran would have eaten it, wouldn't he Mavis? He loves molasses cake."

"Yes, ma, he does," she says softly.

"Save it for him," says Peter, and they both looked at him with indulgent scorn. All the years had blurred but not erased the resentment that Peter had felt when Bran came into their family.

"The surveyors were here again today," says Peter. "That's the third day in a row." Leah shakes her head.

"Were you always in the kitchen, ma?" Mavis asks, knowing the answer but wanting to think about something else.

Leah loved to reminisce about the early days when they first settled the Glade. Nostalgia glows in Leah's eyes as she says, "From the very beginning. Ragnar made it into a game. We had a contest and I won. Of course, Ragnar liked his little jokes and made it out like I lost."

"Did you ever think you would have to leave one day?"

"No, honey, we came for good, wearing all our foolish notions like a tree wears its spring leaves. We never thought anybody would try to force us out. That was the whole idea of the Distribution; to give people a place." Leah's brow knits, her loose lips roll back into her mouth and she growls, "Don't you worry, honey, we're staying put. Our Bran will do what he has to do." Leah reaches across the table and pats Mavis's hand.

The kitchen door opens and the shambling bulk of Thule comes out of the dark. He approaches the table, his gentle eyes shifting from Leah to the square of brown cake. Without asking, he picks it up and takes a bite. His voice muffled, he says, "Petey, I been looking for you. Jock found some cans of gasoline in the brush about ten yards off the road. We figure those surveyors stashed it there."

"What for?" asks Peter.

"Maybe in case they run out of gas." Thule's gaze sharpens. "Or maybe one of them aims to slink back some night and set a fire or two." Thule looks at each of them and chews slowly. "Good cake, Leah."

"We'd better have a guard through the night,"

"You read my mind. Are you willing to work the first shift?"

"Sure, so long as I can carry a loaded shotgun."

Thule nods. "I just hope you don't have to use it."

THE FOURTH DAY

—1—

Bran awakes, not knowing where he is, aware of pain from shoulder to groin, and the remembrance of torture comes throbbing back. The cot on which he is lying is bolted to the wall of a small windowless room painted a uniform shiny grey from floor to ceiling. He sits up and sees that the bed is covered by a blanket and even has a clean pillow on which is printed, "SecureCo". He gets up and goes to the bucket in the corner. It is clean and smells of lye. He uses it; self-consciously aware that some stranger might be watching him through the aperture in the metal door. Moving slowly because of the pain in his shoulder and groin, he puts on his pants and shirt. Humiliation and frustration overcome him as he realizes that for the first time in his life he is confined because he has impetuously risked his life to save a stranger, an enigmatic musician who might be a killer or a smuggler for all he knows. Worst of all, his act has cost him and those who have nurtured him, their home. There is a table and chair in the center of the room, bolted to the floor. He sits down, reads the obscenities scratched on its surface, and hopes that at least Ephus has managed to get away with his pack.

In the corridor beyond the door he hears a rattle of metal, doors opening and slamming at regular intervals. Someone must be coming around with food. As the sounds get louder he patches together a plan of escape. The wall is his only weapon. In the middle of the night he will feign illness and when the guard bends over him he will seize him by the shirt, smash his head against the wall, change into his uniform and leave.

The metal door clicks and opens and an unarmed attendant places a bowl of hot cereal and a white cup of steaming tea on the table. A fly has come into the room with the attendant. He eats, watches the fly's random exploration of the space and wonders if it would ever get out.

As he finishes the cereal the door opens again and a guard says, "Come with me." They lead him down corridors and through doors watched by guards with automatic weapons and his spirits fall as he realizes that without some help he has little chance of escaping. Even so, he takes note of each gate.

"Where are you taking me?" he asks with foreboding as the guard jostles him from behind.

"Court,"

At least it isn't back for more torture. A door opens and he has a moment to blink and look up at the grey sky before he is shoved into the back of a van with several other prisoners. As the van jolts forward, Bran is sickened by the fetid air. He gets up and thrusts his weight against the doors, but they are securely bolted.

The van stops, and with a glimpse of the wall of a grey stone building, Bran and the others are hustled down a corridor and into a high-ceilinged room. The prisoners are seated behind a fence with a side view of what might have been a theater. Chairs arranged in rows face a fence, tables, and what looks to Bran like an altar. The judge has not yet arrived but the room is full of people, some in garish tight fitting clothes, and for the most part looking as if they would rather be someplace else. Behind the bench on a wood paneled wall, he recognizes the standing bear of the Seal of the "California Republic." Under that is a blue shield with crossed keys and the words, "SecureCo". The man next to him looks like the advanced alcoholics that he often saw in Templeton. His skin is almost transparent; waxy and yellow, and the rims of his bloodshot eyes have fallen open.

"What's this SecureCo.?" Bran asks, staring at the shield.

"They runs the place."

"Are they the police too?"

"That's some other outfit. I ferget what they call em. I oughta know," says the man turning toward Bran with a slack lipped grin. "I see'd enough of em."

"All rise," shouts the only man in the room with a gun and everyone gets up to a clatter of chair seats. The judge comes in, wearing a somber black robe that conceals everything but her head. With her blanched face and eyes reduced to pinpoints by thick glasses, the judge looks to Bran like someone specially adapted to this sunless cavern that made up the jail and now the court--a place totally removed from his world of soil, rain, and wind. As if to confuse him, the judge produces from somewhere a small glass vase with six daisies. Placing them in front of her on the desk, she looks around with a wintry smile and gets on with what she calls the "calendar."

Bran watches and listens to the unintelligible ritual with growing fear, as one by one, the prisoners, and many of the people behind the fence, are called forward and intoned over with numbers and obscure language. He listens to the limp explanations, the apologies, the lies, the admissions, as the assailants, panderers, drug dealers, vagrants, and public drunks are extruded either through the door to freedom or the one that leads back to jail. The longer it continues the more he squirms in his seat with anxiety, fearing that this judge, though not lacking in compassion by the look and sound of her, is sure to send him back through the jail door to more torture. With that fixed in his mind he begins again to think about escape. Before getting back in the van, he will kick the guard in the groin, grab his gun and, holding him as a shield, he will disappear into the safety of the *Sal Si Puedes*. A desperate plan but he has nothing to lose.

At the sound of his name his heart plunges into his gut and he moves up to the bench with dread that turns his limbs to wood. The judge gazes down at him through her thick glasses with bird's eyes. Her look is unsympathetic, he imagines, and yet he begins to hope that she will somehow let him go as she has others.

The judge examines some papers in front of her then stabs him with a chillingly solemn gaze and charges him with numbers that translate to assault with the intent to inflict substantial harm on a police officer in the performance of his duties and other things. "How do you plead, Mr. Bran?"

Heart thumping in his throat Bran says haltingly, "It's like I told them last night ..."

She looks impatient, waves her finger at him, and says, "Hasn't this man had the benefit of counsel, Mr. Coe?"

"It's a security issue, your honor. We advanced it."

The judge's pale forehead rumples. "You have a right to remain silent and to be represented by counsel of your own choosing," she says to Bran.

"If you let me go, I promise I'll find one."

Speaking slowly as if she has concluded that Bran is either deaf or slow-witted, she says, "I'm going to send you back to jail and appoint a lawyer to defend you."

Bran grows cold as he hears this, then a rush of anger floods over him and he says, "At least let me try to telephone somebody before you send me back..."

As he says this, he sees the judge looking curiously at something behind him. He is nudged from behind and a voice says, "Plead not guilty and ask for a jury,"

"Mr. Morrison," the Judge says to the man still behind him, "Did more pressing duties keep you from being here on time? Do you represent the accused or are you simply moved by his circumstances?"

"I represent him, your honor, and will enter a not guilty plea and demand a jury."

"Shouldn't you ask the accused about his wishes, or have you added omniscience to your many other skills?"

"That's what I was going to say, Judge." Bran stands there, the suspense stopping the blood in his veins as the lawyers and the judge talk about something called bail. The man who claimed to represent him signs something, and for a moment Bran thinks he is free, at least until the guard and the lawyer motion him toward the door that leads back to jail.

In the corridor, a double door slides open and, together with the lawyer and the guard, he enters another cell. The door shuts and, to Bran's surprise, the cubicle seems to fall. It is Bran's first experience with an elevator. They take him to a long windowless room in which several men are seated in a semi-circle around a television set. Bran sits down on a sofa away from the nasal drone of the TV and for the first time he has a good look at the lawyer; a stout man with broad, sagging shoulders, a thick neck, and a wrinkled face mottled with freckles.

The lawyer quickly explains that he has been hired, "in appreciation for what you did for Nikanor,"

"Then he's alive," says Bran feeling a sense of relief that he hadn't acted for nothing.

"So they tell me."

"Who's they?"

Morrison looks like he doesn't understand the question. Ignoring it he explains that Bran can leave as soon as he gives the court $20,000 to hold until he returns for the next hearing in ten days.

"What if I don't have the money?"

"You stay in jail," says the lawyer looking both weary and apologetic.

Bran bites down on his thumb as he realizes that just getting out of jail would take $2,000 of his Old Dollars, and it could even mean that he wouldn't have enough left to buy the patent. He looks into Morrison's eyes and asks, "Would the same people who sent you, give me, even lend me, the money?"

"Maybe, but it wouldn't be today."

Bran thinks about it for just a moment then he asks Morrison to go to the Hostel and bring back Ephus with his pack. Morrison nods without hesitation and stands up.

"I've got a pre-trial," he says looking at his watch as he leaves the room.

Bran looks around at the greasy looking green walls and the metal chairs with their patched plastic seats. The room is larger than the cell and clean, although the air is stale with cigarette smoke. He is better off than before and grateful for the help. Bran puts aside the thought of a trial that could put him back in jail and concentrates on getting the patent. At worst he stands to lose one day. There is still time. He closes his eyes and imagines a mountain meadow fragrant with young grass and patches of snow on the rocky slopes with nothing more exciting to do than to keep the coyotes away from the sheep. The cackle of the television pulls him out of his day-dream and, despite his unease, he is drawn to the other end of the room. The four other men also waiting to be released are watching a soccer match between West Germany and Belgium.

At the Glade watching TV was discouraged. Ragnar believed that TV eroded the capacity to think. Even so, Bran had often stolen a few minutes in front of the TV at the cafe in Templeton after picking up the mail and had always found it engrossing, even when he hadn't the time to figure out what was happening.

Despite his restlessness he quickly finds himself drawn into the action. Hyde ball, Bran's sport, was a regional adaptation of soccer, but played over a longer time span and with fewer restraints. The game on television is exciting, but to his surprise the others just sit lethargically and watch as though they were in a classroom.

"Did you see that play?" Bran says as a series of passes leads to a tie-breaking goal.

The man next to him manipulates his receded chin and says, "I seen it about a dozen times."

"How's that?"

"The station has a collection of 'em. They play it over and over."

"Don't people get tired of watching it?"

"Naw. You look forward to the good parts."

A guard brings peanut butter sandwiches and something he has never before seen, some thin brown wrinkled discs that gave off a rancid smell. He tastes one and it coats his tongue. His guide with the receding chin tells him that they are potato chips and gladly eats Bran's portion.

Bran asks the guard if he can make a call. "I'll find out," he replies. The men eat, listlessly watching the television set. Bran waits for the guard to return for what seems like an hour. "How can I find out if my lawyer's come back with the bail?" he asks the man next to him.

"You could bang on the door, but it won't do no good."

"Why not?"

"They won't tell you and they won't let you out till after midnight anyhow."

"Why?"

"Because they get paid an extra day's keep from the City if they let us go tomorrow."

"Why would they do that?"

"They get paid by the night. Like a hotel. Where are you from anyhow?" The man looks at him as though he ought to know better.

"Shut up!" says a man on his left, his breath smelling like chicken droppings, "I can't hear the game with all your gassing."

Bran goes to the door and bangs on it. A guard comes and he asks to be taken to the toilet. The corridor is blocked by a locked security door. He asks the guard about his bail and the man promises to look into it. Impatient and frustrated, Bran returns to the holding room and the television.

By the time another guard brings another round of peanut butter sandwiches Bran is suspecting the worst. The lawyer has made off with his money. The pack couldn't be found. It has been taken by the police. The judge has changed her mind. All of these possibilities flap about in his head like agitated bats. To make matters worse his groin muscles are aching and stiff and his shoulder is inflamed.

Again, the TV pulls him back, this time to an appealing blond woman who looks straight into his eyes as she tells him about a house that has burned down after fire trucks from rival companies collided with each other on the way to the fire. There are pictures of the still smoldering gutted house flanked by comfortable houses with landscaping that remind him of the Institute. It is the first time he has seen private houses of such proportion.

"Is this old too?" he asks his neighbor.

"That's the news, man."

The rest of the night is taken up by programs about policemen, sailors, doctors, actresses, rich people, and more policemen. If he hadn't been so impatient, he might have enjoyed the exposure to a universe he'd never seen; sheer walled city streets, skylines that resembled mountain ranges, elegant houses, and murders enough for a whole lifetime. The programs are seamless except that they stop in the middle of the action for little songs and dramatizations of breakfast cereal, soap, clothing, and other products, that had absolutely nothing to do with the substance of the drama.

"Is this stuff new?" he asked with hesitation.

"Naw, it's old, real old. Some of that stuff they don't even sell no more."

The Golden Bear flag of California Republic suddenly flutters in front of clouds; an invisible orchestra plays "California Here I Come" but no one stands up. Two of his three companions are dozing, their heads fallen on their chests like sleeping pigeons. They both start awake as the screen abruptly dissolves into shards of agitated black and white and a distant singer does his best to force his song through the hiss and static.

"It's after midnight," says the man next to him. "They'll be letting us out." Within five minutes someone comes to the door and calls Bran's name. He approaches the guard and is told in a matter-of-fact way that he is free to leave and it is as if someone holding him from behind has suddenly let go.

"What did I tell ya," the man calls to him.

Before releasing Bran, the guard gives him general directions to the *Sal Si Puedes*. A gentle rain is falling, and he stands for a moment watching the trapezoid of light return to the building as the door again closes. He stretches and takes the crisp rain-washed air deep into his chest, wanting to expel every last breath of the stagnant atmosphere of the court. The rain slows as he walks down empty streets watching, with apprehension, the lights of occasional oncoming vehicles. The streets are as dark as the night itself, for there are few overhanging lights, and he has the feeling that, except for an occasional light showing in the window of a house or a dim bulb burning in the rear of a store, he is alone in the world. Having tended sheep in mountain pastures, Bran is at home in the night's opaque solitude. He trots along quietly, meeting only a startled cat along the way.

—3—

He passes storefronts, barred with steel grates behind which could be seen the dim outlines of mannequins, stoves, pots or garden tools. There are cans or bags of trash in front of most stores. Men dressed in the rumpled grey of early dawn are feeding the jaw of a groaning garbage truck. Bran turns down a side street, and after three or four blocks, comes to the end of the pavement. The street empties into a narrow rubble and trash-strewn field, the border of the *Sal*. He enters the passage between two structures, hears a crackling of wheels, and faces a plodding horse, its head drooping as it drags a two-wheeled wagon. Through the stakes of the wagon bed he makes out several bodies lying side by side as if asleep. The sharp angles of their limbs, their half open, retracted eyes, and gaping mouths send a chill through him.

In contrast to the other town, the *Sal* is alive with a reality that resembles the warped, distorted visions of a fever dream. Wherever shelter could be stolen, a shallow doorway, or nothing more than the side of a box leaning against a wall, people sleep. There are derelicts, addicts propped against a wall transfixed in a vacant stupor, the terminally ill in the last throes of life, as well as whole families, men and women without so much as a blanket, their little children sleeping beside them with the ground for a mattress and no more than ragged clothing to cover them. For the first time on his journey, compassion for the homeless clinging by one hand to life overcomes him as he sees the shadow of his own early childhood. Immediately it comes to him that he has his own community to think about, or they would all soon be like these people.

As yet he has seen no one awake or lucid who could direct him to the hostel. He passes an open door and sees, in the frail light of a single candle, six or seven people seated on the floor their backs against the wall. A sweet cloying smell comes out of the place, and he sees that they are alive but inert as wood. A slender man appears out of the shadow. He looks to be in his teens, his blanched skin is stretched taut over his sharp cheekbones and he stares at Bran through round, pale eyes with what might be suspicion or apathy. At last, he says in a whisper, "We got good stuff for you here. You want it?"

A pistol shot, then another, pops somewhere. Bran hears it and flinches. The man in the doorway simply stares at him with eyes of stone.

"I'm looking for St. Procopius."

"He's not here." The man continues to stare, his expression registering nothing, and he slowly turns away.

Revolted, Bran walks on. After about ten minutes in which he thinks that he has walked in a circle, he comes on two children huddled together against a wall. The oldest is about ten. The younger, no more than six, is asleep, his head resting against the shoulder of the other. They are dressed in ill-fitting, ragged clothes and their fair hair is matted and uncombed. Seeing Bran, the older boy looks up with pitiful hope and thrusts out his palm.

"Do you know where the St. Procopius Hostel is?" The child nods solemnly. "I'll pay you if you take me there."

"Can you wait till my brother wakes up? You can't get in anyhow. They lock up and don't open till morning." The child looks at Bran expectantly.

"Sure," and he sits down beside the child and leans back against the wall.

A girl approaches them from out of the shadow, lips cruelly painted, eyes outlined with a dark color so that, even in the night, they seem to reach out of her small head like the lights of a car. Her thin, barely developed torso is covered by a skirt and tight black sweater. Taking Bran for just another street vagrant she walks on, head downcast, eyes fixed on the uneven, muddy surface of the alley.

Again, Bran recalls lonely nights in the high meadows with the sheep and only the rough trunk of a tree to lean against. He is accustomed to discomfort and, despite the ache in his groin and shoulder, the chill now moving from his flesh to his muscles and bones, he does his best to content himself with just this little comforting respite. He imagines Mavis stirring in bed, warm between the sheets under the wool blanket that she had woven, and the memory of her shape arouses motes of longing. Only the shepherds would be awake now, and he wonders where they are and if there has been rain in the mountains. The comforting thoughts of home relax his tired muscles, he almost forgets about his wet clothes, the damp ground, the wall's rough surface and the images dissolve into sleep.

THE FIFTH DAY

—1—

Bran awakes to the boy's prodding of his injured shoulder. There is a hint of light, enough to give substance to the shapes around him but the colors—if this impoverished place has color— are muted.

"The hostel will open soon," the boy says as he helps his brother to his feet. The younger child still has his eyes closed and appears to be frowning, but as he struggles to his feet and simply stands in his place, passive and helpless, Bran sees, with wrenching sympathy, that he is blind. The torture, the night spent on the ground in the rain, has caught up with Bran. Every limb is stiff and he can barely keep from shaking because of the chill. He stretches, stamps his feet, and watches as the older boy, speaking gently to his brother, adjusts his jacket and says, "Come on Charley, we're gonna get some food."

"I'm real hungry, Bobby," says the younger boy.

Bobby wipes his brother's running nose with the sleeve of his coat, takes his hand, and with a gesture of his eyes to Bran, sets out as the grey morning light seeps into the sky. The *Sal Si Puedes* wakes early, and they pass people sitting on the side-walk eating tortillas, and others washing children's faces with water from a public faucet. Soapy water ejects from a doorway, a window opens and an arm extends from a shadow and waters a single geranium. There are sounds; sleep muffled conversation, a mother chastening her children, laughter, and the rank smell of night wastes newly spilled into the streets.

Bran walks along beside the children and listens to the older one encouraging his brother, "Not far now, Charlie."

"Where are your parents, Bobby?" Bran asks, at once regretting it, as he sees the boy's desolate expression.

"I don't know," he says, and his thin lips shut tight.

They reach the wall of the hostel and fall into a line behind others waiting for the gate to open; people of every age, sharing only their impoverishment, dressed in cast off ill-fitting clothes. A few are muttering to themselves, staring inward with rage, and one man, his head wrapped in a yellow turban, is walking up and down the line slapping a guitar without strings. Most of them are simply hungry and groggy from a night spent sleeping on the ground. Five minutes later the gate opens and the line begins to move into the hall passing two priests who greet each one with kind words and a welcoming look.

Bran recognizes one priest and says, "Father Malachi, I'm Bran." The priest looks at him quizzically. His watery eyes widen, and he takes Bran by the elbow, swiftly rakes the line of people with his gaze, and draws him through an arched door. Once they are inside the small room the priest takes him in with admiration and pity.

"You made it back to us." Without waiting for an answer, he hurries back out of the room, the hem of his robe catching for a moment in the closing door. Bran lets himself down into a worn leather chair and wearily drops his head back against the top.

Within a few minutes, the priest returns with a bowl of cereal, a mug of tea, and a brown robe. He puts the tray down on the table next to the chair and gestures to Bran.

"Could you do something for the two boys who brought me here? One is blind," Bran asks before taking the first spoonful of the cereal.

Kindness showing in his eyes, Father Malachi says, "I have seen them. We do what we can for them all."

Before he could say any more the door opens. Ephus bursts into the room and throws himself at Bran. It is as much affection as the boy has ever shown him and Bran is moved by it. When they finally pull apart, Bran asks him if the lawyer had come for his pack and found the money.

Mention of the pack brings on a blush of shame and Ephus stammers, "Some man come for your pack but I told him I didn't have it."

"You were afraid to give it to him?"

His high voice burdened with failure Ephus replies, "Jonah stoled it. But we can get you a new one with the money I got from the cans." He reached into his pocket and produced a few bills.

Bran feels the blood drain out of his head. Looking earnestly from the priest to Ephus, he asks if they knew where Jonas went.

"He just disappeared in the confusion. And when the boy and your friend June looked for your pack after the police finally left, they found that it was missing. One of the priests thinks that he saw him leaving with it."

"You're sure the police didn't take it?"

"I would have seen them." Father Malachi touches Bran's shoulder. "I'm sure that we can help to replace your belongings."

Bran looks up at him outwardly calm yet feeling an icy grip on his heart. Somehow, he has to find Jonah and the money or the Glade is lost. He can't do it alone, if at all, but he has to try. Begin with the priest, he tells himself. "Who got me out of jail?"

"Friends of Nikanor."

Bran takes a deep breath and tells the priest about the money in the pack and what it is for. The priest listens, fingering the black wooden cross that hangs around his neck. When Bran has finished, he replies without hesitation, "Nikanor will do what he can for you. I'm certain of that. I will make arrangements to have you taken to him. In the meantime, put this on, and put your trust in God." he says, handing Bran the cassock.

After he has left the room, Ephus asks, "Can't you buy whatever you need with this?" He offers the money a second time.

"Thanks pal, but it's a few dollars short," Bran replies, roughing the boy's hair.

Blinking back tears, Ephus says, "I let you down."

"No you didn't. Now help me get my shirt off and tell me what happened to June. Did she leave?"

Ephus brightens and tells him that June is still staying at the Hostel. "But she got into trouble 'cause they put her in with the girls." Bran has to smile at that.

—2—

Father Malachi returns, followed by June looking carelessly lovely, her hair falling in loose waves about her cheeks, the faded blue shirt open to the cleavage of her breasts. She runs to Bran, kisses him on the cheek and gives him a quick hug.

"So now you're a priest," she says tossing her hair back from her cheek and giving a whinny of a laugh. "I'm glad I saw you before I left. Someone came with my picture, but Father Malachi put him off." She smiles at the priest with affectionate gratitude and his already rosy complexion seems to deepen.

"This is a sanctuary; which is why they often begin the hunt here."

"You already know that Jonah stole your pack."

Bran is doing his best to maintain his composure, but the theft of the pack is plunging him deeper and deeper into despair. Briefly, he tells her about his frustrated mission, and June reacts with sympathy and a willingness to help. He takes her hand and says, "What could you do but get yourself caught."

"We could look for him."

"He probably got the first bus to anywhere."

A quiet knock on the door interrupts their melancholy discussion. Father Malachi unbolts it and a young priest whispers something to him.

"They've already come for you, Bran."

Bran looks at Ephus and says, "Wait for me. I'll be back for you," and the boy responds with tight-lipped dejection.

He turns to June and she says with a wry shrug, "I'll probably be gone when you get back."

"I hope we'll meet again."

Father Malachi takes him by the arm and hustles him down corridors through a larder stocked with food and out a door to the delivery entrance. An old, grey panel truck with the word "Scavenger's" on the side is waiting with its motor running, and a black man, with hair tied in many little braids, is lounging against the open driver's door, smoking a cigarette. The priest looks at the van. He seems to verify something, he turns to Bran and says, "Go with him, and God be with you."

"Please get in the back and put this around your eyes," the man says handing Bran a white cloth. Bran hesitates. "It's for your own good and ours." Bran climbs in, sits down on the dusty floor, and puts the blindfold on. The van drives for a long time, turning frequently. Although the driver often sings to himself, he says nothing to Bran. As he sits there jarring against the wall, the more he sifts the possibilities of retrieving the money, the more hopeless it seems. Even assuming that by some miracle Jonah could be found, the chance of it happening in the next few days is remote. He can already feel shame as he faces all of those who loved and trusted him. He resolves to try anything, take any risk, to find Jonah. Even if he must track him like a sheep-killing coyote across the whole country, he will make him pay for his theft.

The truck's abrupt halt shakes him out of his thoughts. Still blindfolded, Bran is led down a long flight of stairs along a cool corridor. The blindfold is removed, and he finds himself in a windowless room facing Nikanor. Dressed in blue coveralls, Nikanor is standing in front of a simple oak table strewn with papers, his violin and bow in hand as though he has just been playing. The room is simply furnished but with a few touches of warmth; a small Persian rug with a geometric design on a maroon field, two moss green armchairs and a small vase of fresh violet and purple petunias. One wall is covered with books on shelves from floor to ceiling. Nikanor's pale blue eyes reach toward him with welcome, as he gently puts his violin back in its case and puts his arm around Bran's shoulder. "How are you feeling, brother?"

"Like a butchered sheep," Bran replies, staring at him with respect. Nikanor's self-possession, his command, is even more apparent in what Bran takes to be the secret headquarters of

Unity America. Nikanor pours each of them a glass of brandy. At his insistence, Bran bolts it down, feels its warm trail as he repeats his story.

"How much time do you have to get the patent?"

"Just five more days,"

"Boy!" says Nikanor and he snaps upright in his chair. "We'll start today; scour all the places where he's likely to be. We'll check every bed if we have to."

"How do you figure on doing that?"

"Do you know anything about Unity America?"

"I'd never heard of it before the police, Nikanor."

"Well, let me tell you a little so you'll understand why they tortured you and why they let you out. With that introduction, Nikanor explains that Unity America is a shadow government that does some of what government used to do before the Dissolution; providing money for hospitals to care for the needy, money to support the destitute, classes for children who lacked the money to pay tuition for their education, and job training for out-of-work adults.

More interested in the search for Jonah, Bran listens with only half an ear. Out of politeness he asks, "Where do you get the money for all this?"

"We raise taxes from businesses in the cities."

"So why are the police after you?"

Nikanor attempts an angelic expression. "I sometimes can't sleep nights wondering about that myself."

Bran shrugs and looks perplexed through the fog of his distraction. Just one more crazy way the world was. The founders of the Glade were right to have nothing to do with it. "How are we going to find Jonah?"

"If he's in town, we know where to look for him. We can get a thousand pairs of eyes if we have to; the bus stations, stores where he might spend his money, food stands. All we need is a good identification."

They try to construct a description of Jonah, but it soon becomes apparent that, aside from the most general awareness of his height and age and the fact that he has a longish face, they couldn't even agree on the color of his eyes. What they had fit hundreds of derelicts. "What about Ephus, is he observant?"

"He's real sharp," says Bran, "and he could walk the streets and look for him. So could June for that matter if she wasn't running away herself. Maybe if you brought them here, we could all put together a description."

"There's a problem. Very few people are permitted to come to this place. I bent the rules to bring you here as it was. It's just what the police would have wanted me to do." Nikanor turns away from him and paces the room.

"If you won't bring them here, then take me back to the Hostel and I'll try to find Jonah; Ephus and me." Resolution hardens Bran's features. Nikanor turns away, leans over the desk and drums his fingers.

"If you put it that way," Nikanor says, with a shrewd, bemused expression. "I'll send someone to bring them both here." Nikanor dispatches a driver to pick up the others, gives Bran a simple history of the United States to read and leaves him alone.

—3—

He walks down a long concrete corridor past doors marked only with initials and numbers, behind which can be heard the buzz or stamp of machinery, the single voice of a lecturer, or music from a radio.

He uses his key, one of fifteen that opens door H-2, and enters a long room brightly lit by overhead florescent lights, dominated by a conference table of polished walnut. One wall is covered with maps, some of the California Republic, others of cities, and one section has nothing but photos and plans of the Standard refinery at San Pedro. Two people, a man and a woman, both middle-aged, are sitting next to each other at the table, heads bent over some papers. The man is squarely built, his large head is planted on broad shoulders and is dominated by a thick crown of grey hair which contrasts with heavy black eye brows and deep-set, intelligent eyes, as black as coal.

"Cris," says Tom, "Nice of you to drop in. I understand you brought us another stray." Cris is short for Crispus, Nikanor's name on the Committee of the Whole. Crispus Attuks was the first black to die in the cause of the American Revolution.

"I owe that stray my life, Tom." Nikanor gazes at him with indulgent affection. He is accustomed to Tom's sharp tongue and knows him to be kind and gentle under his horny shell.

"He's a member of a big club then."

Betsy puts her hand on Tom's to quiet him. She is a slender woman. Her hair is grey with a suggestion of blond, her wrinkled skin stretched thin over fine cheek bones. Only her clear eyes, slate grey and large, show no sign of age.

"We need at least ten hours of your time, Cris, before you go to Los Angeles, if you persist in going." She has a clear voice crazed from years of smoking and she polishes her words, a carry-over from her New England Brahmin family.

"You've developed the attention span of a fly, Cris, over the years," says Tom, his voice nasal and harsh.

"You ain't what you was either." Nikanor drops into a chair across from them and pours some coffee from a carafe on the table. "I've got to go, Bet. You know that. If I don't, Rudolpho and the radicals will take full credit for the job and there'll be no holding them back. That's why I've got to go down there whether I want to or not. You know as well as I do that the Chicano's want their own country from Los Angeles to the border."

"And only you can keep them from splitting away from Unity and forming their own Spanish speaking organization," says Tom his voice tainted by skepticism.

"For the time being that's my belief."

"And what have we done to develop loyal regional leaders who will one day replace you as a cult figure?"

"Rudolpho started out that way. They all did. But they have their own way of seeing things." Nikanor looked from one to the other, his pale eyes calm, almost innocent, hiding the fatigue. Tom is right, he thinks. No sooner did you build a group than it went its own way. Almost to himself he adds, "You can't blame them for developing their own ideas. They're human beings, not robots. Isn't that what democracy's supposed to be all about? You can't blame them for losing patience or for wanting to go their own way."

"Unfortunately, Cris, their independence no longer includes a commitment to democracy as you and I understand it." Tom hunches his shoulders forward and clasps his hands together. "There are even rumors afoot that they've got your name on one of their lists. They reason that with you out of the way, the Militants can get complete control of Los Angeles."

"Yeah, I heard that too."

Betsy looks across the table at Nikanor. "It's just another reason for you not to participate in the raid on the refinery. A stray bullet might have your name on it."

Nikanor tilts his head and pulls his full lips back. If he feels fear, he can't acknowledge it. "What's that saying? I can take care of my enemies, but God protect me from my friends. Besides, maybe at this point I'm worth more dead than alive." His eyes focus on the papers in front of Betsy. "What have you got there?"

"Allocations for the next quarter. Feel like going over them?

"No. But I will anyhow."

—4—

Bran stares at the book Nikanor had given him but his mind is churning the mud of his problem. Rather than sit out a futile search for Jonah, it might be better to return to the Glade and see if something else might be done. Maybe the Counsel could find some other land.

Nikanor comes into the room. "I know what you're thinking; that it's like trying to find the fox that stole the chicken. Well, it is. But it can be done."

"I don't know. Jonah's always on the move. If I was him, I'd of gotten on the first bus out of here."

"Not necessarily. Put yourself in his place. He knows you can't get out of jail when you almost kill a policeman. So he can sit tight in Fresno if he wants to."

"How did I get out?"

"They must have thought that you'd lead them to me."

"I guess you must be pretty important."

"Maybe to them."

Someone brings them two peanut butter sandwiches on wheat bread and a pot of herb tea. Bran is hungry and eats both sandwiches while Nikanor sits at the table and begins to read some papers, making notes in the margin. Anxious and feeling pent in by the windowless room, Bran gets up and starts to pace, stopping to look at every object with distraction, then passing on to the next. After five minutes of this Nikanor looks up from his work and said, "Do you play chess?"

"Nope."

Nikanor puts his pencil in a glass on the table and asks Bran about the Glade. Bran tells him about its isolation and describes the simple way of life. "Why is everybody so poor except for the fenced towns like the one where we first met you?" Bran asks.

Incredulity washes Nikanor's features and he says, "They really didn't tell you anything up there at the Glade." He sits down in the other armchair. "The Big Parch started with a twenty-year drought compounded by an earthquake that damaged a nuclear reactor and spread radiation. About the same time the United States was breaking up, there was an epidemic of a drug-resistant flu that started in Los Angeles. Because people in the other part of the land didn't want to be affected by the sickness, they quarantined California. They wouldn't let people out. They thought that the sickness could be passed on to the children and they didn't want that to happen."

"Were they right? Could it be passed on that way?"

Nikanor gets up and goes to the library shelves as if they might have the answer. "Not really. But eventually they just made the quarantine permanent, which is why there are all of these inspection stations and the buses don't go very far. Later they passed out the public land to compensate people who remained. Then they began sending criminals here or dissidents; people who didn't fit in, and it became a place of exile as well. It was easier and cheaper to ship a criminal to California and let them go than support them in prison. Now you know a little about your home."

"What about east of the mountains. What's it like there?"

"A little like here but not as bad. There are lots of poor but more help for them. More jobs, places where things are made. More people who are neither rich nor poor. People have more money and they buy more so the stores have more goods. If we have the time I'll give you some books that tell about it." Nikanor goes on with his explanation and he is still talking about the way things are east of the mountains when Ephus and June come into the room.

"You were almost too late," June says. "I was within about five minutes of taking a bus to Los Angeles."

"Sorry."

She returns a free smile. "I'd just as soon be here. I'd say it's safer than a bus."

Nikanor and Bran fill them in, and within a few minutes they have agreed on a description of Jonah. Ephus recalls the color of his eyes, his peculiar long teeth and June is even able to sketch a reasonably faithful profile.

—5—

"The description and drawing will be on the street this afternoon," says Nikanor, rubbing the socket of his eye with his knotted fist.

Bran purses his lips and looks down at his shoes, then looks at Nikanor with resolution and says, "Me and Ephus are going to look for him on the street in the meantime."

With a pale, sober look, June says, "I'll go too."

Nikanor shakes his head and mutters ruefully, "I guess I've got to go with you since I'm the only one who knows where to look and what to do if we find him. I'll be dressed as a minister. June, we'd better do something about you as well."

"What do you have in mind, a nun's habit to complete the theme?"

"Too much of anything can be harmful, even religion," Nikanor quips, his blue eyes suddenly flashing. "How about a waif; some ragged clothes, a hat to cover that lovely hair, some dirt on the face?"

"As long as they're clean, and don't smell as bad as they look. And no lice."

"All clean and fumigated, I promise." Nikanor escorts June to a room across the hall, his own bedroom, and has the clothes brought to her. Twenty minutes later they look at each other the way children in costume admire one another. With his large gold cross, his curly grey beard, and metal-rimmed glasses, Nikanor is greatly changed while June, wearing drab, patched pants, and a grey oversized shirt, is still charming to see, even with the smudged face and grey makeup under her eyes. A wisp of a wave escapes from her moth-eaten cap and dangles over her forehead, and the drab clothes only accentuate by contrast the devilish energy beaming from her eyes.

Again, they put on the blindfolds and are led up the stairs to the van. A curtain is pulled across the front of the compartment to block the view and they remove the blindfolds. As the van jounces along, Nikanor explains that they will be searching an area of the *Sal Si Puedes* called the "Warren." People running from something stay there. Every building houses a hotel above the street. At the street level there are cafes where the residents play cards, dice, or dominoes, and stores where stolen goods are bought and sold. "You can even hire your own squad of street toughs to protect you."

"You think Jonah's done that?" asked Bran.

Nikanor sneezed. "The dust in here gets to me. They ought to clean this van once in a while. That would just call attention to him." He reaches into a black satchel and produces a map and a supply of cigarettes and matches. "This will get you in and out. The area to search is marked. And you can sell the matches and cigarettes in the cafes," he says to Ephus and June. "You can keep what you make," he adds with an open grin.

"What do we do if we see him?" asks June.

"One of you go to Doodle's Café; it's marked on the map here. Tell Doodle, a short bald man with jowls, that Nikanor needs a pickup. He'll send three men with you. They'll be waiting there. Bran and I will visit as many of the hotels as we can. You will be picked up by this same van, here," he says pointing to an intersection on the map. "Don't get there too early or too late. It's just outside the *Sal* across from the Southern Bus Station and it's not safe for vagrants."

The van stops and Ephus and June get out, then it moves on a few more blocks before dropping Nikanor and Bran on a side-street of metal-working shops. They walk past open workshops, bright with sparks from metal cutting torches, the clangor of hammers on steel and the shrill rip of a saw. They cross a muddy field, derelict with piles of rotting, fly-swarmed garbage, fetid with the smell of excrement, and approach the collapsing stucco walls and despondent windows of the labyrinth.

The narrow, malodorous lanes of the *Sal* teem with people competing for their small measure of sustenance. Beggars, their milky eyes turned inside out, crowd together. Others stand immobile in grotesque frozen poses. They pass people with arms that taper off at the elbow or with no arms at all, being fed by women in simple grey dresses. The concentration of misery shocks Bran and he finds himself wanting to close it off, and yet drawn to it as passers-by an accident can't help staring.

Bran walks at Nikanor's side, somehow hopeful that this mysterious leader of a shadow organization might retrieve his money. He thought of the man's air of authority masked by his easy-going manner. Sought by the police he is walking openly in the streets. But Nikanor could have the excitement and uncertainty of his life. His own life is better than Nikanor's. A cool drink on the porch, watching the sunset after a day's work is all he would ever want. Understanding everything you can see around you is contentment.

Someone bumps against him and he recoils, feeling hemmed in by the crowd. Ahead, people are gathered around a juggler—he can see the bright red and blue pins flying up—and hadn't they just passed a clown? He has seen laughter on faces. In the bright sunlight more people look healthy than sick, and there is an intensity about the bargaining. People walk along conversing, arguing, trying to sell everything from a cake to a razor. There are so many different people and languages. Bran recognizes Spanish and one that sounds like nasal singing turns out to be Chinese. As for the clothing, everyone who can afford to seem to express something of themselves in their dress; everything from loose fitting white dresses with bright embroidered flowers on the breast to tight semi-transparent body stockings in strange colors worn by men and women lounging in doorways. Several men are wearing wide-brimmed felt hats and black shiny boots with long pointed tips and heels and a dark woman is wearing a long skirt, made of purple and brown silk that wraps around her shoulder and chest. The diversity is stimulating and Bran begins to understand how, even with all of its uncertainty and danger, some people might prefer this to the placid, even boring, life of the Glade. These impressions are all he gets. Although they go into a dozen dark hotel corridors smelling of stale cooking odors, rat droppings, and despair, they learn nothing about Jonah.

—6—

While Bran and Nikanor canvas the likely hotels, June and Ephus scan the cafes and card shops. Blending invisibly with the other ragged young people on the streets, staying within sight of each other, they try to attract as little attention as possible as they observe the poker players or the men hunched over an empty cup staring vacantly at an old book. Except for a middle-aged man wearing an ill-fitting hairpiece who approaches June and offers to buy her a meal, no one speaks to them. Looking about her, June has the sense that people, especially the vendors, view strangers either with suspicion or expectation. It is as if they want to know whether to fear them or what might be sold to them, dismissing them from sight and mind as soon as it becomes apparent that it is neither. She has the illusion that she is invisible, that any compassion that strangers might have felt for the homeless or the sick has simply been walled up--there is so much poverty all around.

The afternoon passes quickly and when she looks at the cheap watch that Nikanor has given her, she sees that they should make their way to the pick-up point. June locates Ephus, catches his attention, and gestures with her arm. They walk out of the immediate foot- traffic into the shadow of a lane, stopping next to a woman washing clothes in a galvanized bucket in front of a low door. June unfolds the map and they study it together to determine the shortest path to the rendezvous. Ephus quickly lays out a route with his finger and leads her through the many turns to the designated place, about a hundred yards from the compound that houses the buses traveling south. The corner where they are to be picked up is an area of small workshops open to the street. In contrast to their anonymity inside the *Sal*, Ephus and June look out of place among the blue and brown denim-clad laborers. June looks at the watch and sees that they have ten minutes to wait. She remembers Nikanor's warning and thinks about returning to the security of the *Sal* but decides against it, since the truck could come early and leave without them.

A few trucks pass, but none that meet the description. Ephus has gone into an alley to pee and June is turning over the events of the day when a truck passes and comes to a stop. It doesn't exactly meet the description, but it is a panel truck. When two men get out of it and come toward her, she assumes that it is their ride, and walks toward them calling out to Ephus. The men are tall, heavy set, and wearing dark blue coveralls. As she closes on them something in their expressions, the stalking look of a hunter, makes her hesitate, but too late. Alarmed, she turns and runs only to be tackled from behind. She sprawls on the pavement, lunges forward, but is restrained by a crushing hammerlock around her neck and the weight of the man's heavy body on top of her. She chokes out a stifled scream of rage, kicks, tries to pull him over her head, but her struggles only tighten the strangle-hold. They drag her struggling toward the truck as June, on the edge of passing out, fights for air. She is dimly aware of sprawling on the metal floor of a dark, foul-smelling hutch. The space is too low to stand up but she struggles to a crouch and slams her shoulder against the door. The truck lurches forward and when her eyes have adjusted to the dark she sees that she is not alone. With her are two skeletal men who lie on the floor unconscious, and fear, bordering on terror, convulses her.

Ephus comes out of the alley, startled to see June flung like a sack into the back of a van. He watches, feeling rage and helplessness. Several people pass the truck and, if they see what has happened, show no sign of it. He mentally records all the details; the clothes of the men, the color of the truck, even the initials printed in black on the side. He watches it drive off, feeling ashamed that just as he has been unable to protect Bran's pack, he has abandoned June. If he had been beside her, he might have sensed the danger and they could have run into the thicket of the *Sal* and escaped. She has risked her life for him and he has failed her. He remains in the shadow of the wall until the truck is out of sight. Dreading his meeting with Bran, he slips into the sunlight as an otter slides into water and his eyes are everywhere at once.

—7—

"June's been took!" Ephus blurts out as he climbs into the van and hearing it, Bran feels his stomach twist with self-blame. He sits on the bouncing floor of the panel truck, silent, his lips pressed together, his arms wrapped around his legs as a dejected Ephus tells them the details.

"You're sure the letters on the truck are LCA?" Nikanor asks.

"I know letters." says Ephus.

"What's it mean?" asks Bran.

"It's the Labor Contractor's Association." He says no more until Bran prods him for an explanation. Then he speaks with long distracted pauses. "They put healthy people to work; contract them out to labor camps and other places. The sick and old, they give an injection, put them to sleep painlessly. Then they take their blood, their healthy organs, and sell them. The rest they burn for fertilizer."

Bran's stomach writhes at the image and he finds himself shouting, "Why didn't you warn her about it?"

"There's no danger inside the *Sal*. They're afraid to go in there because they're hated and they usually don't come out alive."

"Can we get her out?"

"As soon as we get back, I'll send somebody down there to buy her contract. It won't be a problem. They keep them for a day or so before they do anything. Don't worry about her." Nikanor rubs his forehead as if he has a headache. "The worst thing that will happen tonight is that they will put her through a delousing."

Bran reaches out and touches Ephus's head, feeling his soft light hair as if to reassure himself that the boy is still beside him. Ephus takes his hand and holds it firmly. They might have taken Ephus as well, he thinks. His life has become so complicated and it all came back to Nikanor. For a moment he finds himself regretting his rescue attempt. Life wasn't just a game of hyde ball; there are no rules, and you can't walk away from a bad play. You are stuck with it, stuck forever. At the Glade they had warned him against getting tied up with strangers. Yet they had all been helpful. Even Jonah had fixed his shoulder. The van lurches and throws them against the truck wall. Bran's indignation yields to a glow of sympathy for Nikanor. He has no idea what Nikanor does, except that he risks his life to help others just as Ragnar had reached out to him on the road. Nikanor is like Ragnar, a leader of others who gave of himself.

"It's not your fault, Nikanor. You don't make things happen."

"I sure try to," says Nikanor with the embryo of a laugh.

They fall silent in the dusty confinement of the bouncing truck. Then abruptly, Bran asks, "Is it always this bad?"

"Just hope that it won't be worse tomorrow."

—8—

The moment they return to Unity America's headquarters, Nikanor dispatches someone to buy June's contract from the Labor Contractor's Association. The three of them sit down at Nikanor's table to a meal and a wait of the kind endured by passengers who arrive at a bus stop with the suspicion that the last bus has come and gone.

The messenger returns after two hours, a troubled look on his round face. "They refused to give her up," he says, extending his arms palms outstretched in a gesture of incomprehension. "The guy says she's already been taken. When I pushed him he got suspicious and started to ask me some questions."

"What kind of questions?" Nikanor asks. He is holding his violin, a grave stare fixed on the man's wide, confused eyes.

"What you'd expect. I told him we'd already hired her and a kid saw them take her away. Then it took me an hour to lose them after I left."

"Did you see her?" Bran asks.

Nikanor returns his violin to his case, carefully folding the soft cloth around it. The others watch him as, slightly stooped and rubbing his chin thoughtfully, he walks about the room as a caged animal measures its confinement. At length he looks up, fixes his gaze on his assistant, and says, his voice calm and resonant, "Anybody from the relief squad around?"

"Dan and Jo Linne."

"Tell them to stay around. And get some quick paint on the panel truck."

"What color this time?"

"The Labor Contractor Association. What color, Ephus?"

The boy's face brightens with the satisfaction of being included and he says with authority, "Blue, dark blue."

"And get us all some coveralls."

"You going too, Nikanor?" the man asks, surprise showing on his face.

"You know the rules; everybody cleans up their own mess. This is my mess."

The man glares at Nikanor. Seeing the look, Nikanor breaks into an unexpected smile of affection. "George, see that we all have loaded canisters of April Flower. We'll go as soon as the paint's dry. No. Make that as soon as the letters are on the truck. It'll dry on the way."

With a weary shrug and a sigh, George leaves the room. Bran looks at Nikanor feeling new respect for him. The tide of pregame eagerness is restoring his energy and hope. It makes no difference that going out after June is dangerous and won't help recover the stolen money. What matters is that they are acting against the other team, the strangers who, for reasons he doesn't understand, are thwarting him and his companions. It is his way of dealing with problems, the only way he knows; push back with all your strength and will. Nikanor is so decisive, so different from the old men at the Glade who couldn't make up their minds on anything until it was too late.

Nikanor looks at him. "You've cheered up, I see. You must think we'll find Jonah at the L.C.A."

"No, it's just that we're doing something."

"I know what you mean. It may not always be the right thing, but at least it feels good to act," Nikanor replies, and they exchange a look of understanding.

A tall man with a broad, deeply creased forehead and long arms returns with blue coveralls, and Nikanor and Bran pull them on while Ephus looks on with suspicion. "Do I get to go too?"

"Sure you do. We've got to have a reason to go there. And you're it. We're going to take you there and hopefully bring you back."

"Why do you think they won't let her go?" asks Bran.

Nikanor shakes his head, "My guess is the Institute got the word out to pick her up and bring her back. They must get some of their people from the Labor Contractor's in the first place."

Bran looks at Ephus and his spine contracts with the thought that the boy would have been a captive if June hadn't helped free him.

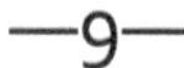

As Nikanor and the others prepare to rescue June, Clement Bigbe, the Night Superintendent of the Labor Contractors Association is trying to decide what to do with her. A short man with thick, wrinkled skin, Bigbe is sitting at his metal desk in his small office looking over reports when his assistant Phil Pariso comes through the open door to announce that June is definitely the, "girl the Institute wants put away." Pariso is sweating in his blue coveralls, and he pulls a large red bandana out of his pocket and wipes his forehead.

"Jack and Tim just picked her up thinking she is a vag hanging around the bus zone. It's our lucky day." Bigbe stops to pick at the scab on a razor nick on his chin. "What do we do now? dismantle, sell the parts and get the premium from the Institute?"

Pariso pours tea into his cracked blue cup from a glass carafe, sits down on the armless aluminum chair and says, "It would be like putting away a money-winning race horse, Hank." His greasy brown eyes brightened. "We stripped her down for the delousing and she's perfect. We could get ten thousand dollars, maybe more, for her from a brothel in New Orleans. She's pretty wild but we would dope her up until she settled down."

Bigbe's loose lips flop forward as he looks down at his desk wondering whether it would be worth the risk to violate Dr. Shiksal's trust–he is after all a good account. But Shiksal has asked too much. They only dispose of the aged and weak; that is the policy. This is a waste of a good resource and chances are he would never find out about it if we shipped her far enough.

"Let me have a look at her," Bigbe says as he gets up and trundles to the door, followed by his assistant. His office opens up into what looks to be a hospital treatment room with its white walls and glaring overhead lights. Immaculate stainless-steel tables, white painted cabinets filled with chemicals in brown bottles, syringes, and shiny surgical instruments; scalpels, even stainless steel saws for cutting through bone announce that here, people having first been drugged, are drained of blood and dissected. They go through another door into a hot corridor, dimly lit and smelling of disinfectant. The area resembles a kennel lined as it is with metal lattice doors enclosing cells no more than six feet by four feet. Each cell has nothing but a wooden sleeping platform raised two inches off the concrete floor, a galvanized bucket filled with water, and in the corner, an open sewer drain. It is here that they house what they call the terminal cases.

Bigbe passes emaciated men and women stretched out on the pallets, unmoving, and he thinks that nothing but fertilizer could be recovered from these wretched husks. White knuckles and fingers grip and shake the grate of one cell, and he turns to see a knotted face with teeth bared and raging wild eyes that make him recoil. That one would bring a good price when all the parts are added up, he thinks, for the totally crazy ones are usually the best physical specimens. He feels right about ridding the streets of ones like that; they can be so destructive. The man begins shrieking obscenities in a rasping barely human voice, and Bigbe hears the splatter of water on concrete and knows that the nut is urinating through the grate. That disposal will be a true public service.

June's cell is at the end of the corridor, and he peers in obliquely so as not to block the light from the overhead bulb in the hall. She is sitting on the sleeping platform, leaning against the wall, her nude body angled away from the door, legs bent at the knee and tucked under, her arms folded, partially covering her breasts. Bigbe admires the swelling of her hips and buttocks, the narrow waist and fine tapered torso. She turns a scornful, side-wise glance toward him and looks away.

Bigbe says nothing to June. It is against the rules to speak to the terminal patients. Limited contact makes putting them to sleep easier. After noting mentally that it would be a shame to destroy such a perfect specimen, he nods approvingly to his assistant and walks back down the hall. Avoiding the puddle of pungent smelling urine, he wonders if they could get away with contracting June to a distant brothel.

The panel truck, its paint still tacky, has already pulled into the yard of the Labor Contractors Association and stopped near the door identified as the "Receiving Entrance". Four people wearing blue coveralls flank the metal door. One of them has Ephus tethered by a lead around his neck. Nikanor tries the door, finds it locked, and rings the service bell. He gestures with his eyes to Bran, who immediately presses against the wall out of sight, as does Dan on the opposite side. Bran's heart is thumping in his throat, and he wonders what if no one comes to the door.

He hears a metallic click, the door opens, and he holds his breath as he has been told to do. He sees Nikanor raise his arm as if to shake the hand of the person still inside the corridor. The spray from the little canister clutched in Nikanor's palm is soundless. Almost instantly the man's legs collapse out from under him and Bran turns toward the door to see him sprawled on the floor, his eyes open but sightless.

They pause long enough to exchange smiles then move down the hall toward the half open door to the "Autopsy Room". Nikanor cautiously pushes the door open and sees that it is empty. He gestures to the others with his hand and they follow behind him and fan out. Knowing what is done in this place, Bran looks around at the instruments and bottles, horrified by the cold sterility.

Nikanor is walking toward a grey steel door with an inset window when it opens, and Bigbe comes into the room looking startled and perplexed as he sees what seem to be four employees and a boy they have brought in. Nikanor walks up to him like a new employee, a toothy smile spread across his face. Muscles tense, Bran freezes, eager to leap to Nikanor's aid and admiring his self-control. As if to shake Bigbe's hand Nikanor extends his arm and Bigbe looks down as the spray mists toward him. Like the other man he collapses within seconds.

"The door!" Bran shouts as he sees it slam and he bolts forward and hits it with his good shoulder. He wrenches the knob against the pressure of the man he sees through the small window. "Lunge when I say!" Bran shouts without looking, as gradually he wrenches the knob around, freeing the latch. "Now!" he says, and together he and Nikanor batter the door open, slamming Pariso against a cell.

Nikanor gets to him first, grabs him by the throat, and smashes his head against the wall. "Give me the keys to the cells," he says his voice low and menacing, "or I'll paralyze you." Bran trots past him looking in each cell and calling out, "June!" Excited by the commotion several old people pull themselves up and stare uncomprehendingly while the disturbed man looking wildly frightened, begins to scream. Above the din Bran hears June's dusty voice shout, "I'm down at the end!" He rushes toward her.

"Keep watch out there!" Nikanor shouts to the others still in the autopsy room. "There may be more workers in the building." Pariso fumbles with the keys and surrenders them. Nikanor lets go of him with a final shake and catches up to Bran.

"Better hurry before somebody alerts the police. Which key?"

"Fourteen," Pariso shouts back.

June stands clutching the cell door. Bran rages inside against those who have caged June like an animal. As Nikanor fumbles for the key and opens the door, June flies through the opening and into Bran's arms, where she clings for only a moment as if to assure herself that this is real. All she says is, "Oh," but the expression tells Bran everything.

"Should we let some of these others out?" Bran asks after June pulls away.

Nikanor is already running down the hall. "No time," he shouts. He pauses only to spray the assistant who, looking stunned, melts to the floor. "Hold your breath," he says to June as she approaches, and the three of them spill out of the door into the bright Autopsy Room and run down the corridor to the outside. The motor of the van is idling and the driver is already in gear as they tumble through the rear doors. When the truck is moving Bran and Nikanor look at each other and let out ecstatic whoops. Bran looks at June, knees up against her chest, and sees her brimming relief as a sputter of laughter yields to choked sobs.

Nikanor finds a small tarpaulin, and hands it to her saying, "Sorry, but that's all we've got. We didn't think to bring you some clothes." Still sobbing and trembling from the effort to control it, she nods and wraps it around her body. Her voice, a bitter contralto, caught through her sobs, she says, "I hope you killed those bastards."

"Sorry June but we don't believe in killing. It's just temporary paralysis."

"Too bad."

"They will have a headache that will make them think they've been hit by a truck if that's any satisfaction to you."

A winsome smile appears through the tears. "Better than nothing."

Bran looks at her, glad that she is safe, pleased to have helped, and for the time being he forgets completely about the theft of the money.

—10—

Mavis watches a bashful moon hide behind a gauze scarf trailing across the night sky. Five days now the moon has waned, and five days she has lived without Bran, her mate. To say she has lived without him is not true for he has been in her mind constantly to the point of distraction. Everyone has noticed it, especially Leah and her brother, Peter, even the little children, who she regularly cares for while their parents are working. Only today, Steven, one of her favorites, asked her something. She hadn't answered, and he had said with his usual directness and quaintness of expression, "When are you coming back, Mavis?"

It was a gift, although to her it seemed more a disability, to have what Ragnar had called a "traveling spirit." Mavis was responsible for the celebrations that marked the seasons. This observance, not yet a ritual, was little more than a focus on the cycle of decay and renewal of life. The first sign of color on the branches of a tree after a long winter, the first rain, the first vegetable, the end of harvest, all are occasions for song, dance, and special meals, with extra honey on bread and cake for the children. The celebrations are never quite the same, but certain songs and snatches of poetry were repeated because someone remembered or liked them. Mavis's spirit, her neighbors believe, is somehow in tune with the elemental forces of life. An impulse, not unlike desire, tells her when planting should take place, and as now, an unfocused fear is warning her that things are not in order. She has more than one reason to be afraid, she thinks as she leans back against the sharp edge of the post that supported her porch roof. Mavis is not a worrier. But every day now men came through the Glade on the way to the mine site, and just two days ago Ivar and Thule had barely stopped a heavy truck pulling a yellow bulldozer on a flatbed trailer, as it was about to traverse the lane across the Glade. The driver had cursed, but turned away as Ivar, a husky dairyman who stood better than six feet, threatened to drive his pitchfork through the truck's tires.

Past midnight, she thinks, as the moon hatches from a ghostly cloud and steadies itself in a dark hole in the night sky. Caleb, Bran's long-haired Shepherd, is stretched out at her side, his long-nosed head resting on his paws. The air is crisp as new apples with its sharp warning of fall. The ground exudes an overripe fragrance since the first rains brought on the decay of dead grass. The harvest celebration is just a week away. She has even written a new song for the children. All the cabins in the Glade are dark. She and Peter, who is on watch, are the only two people awake. The guard duty, rotated among the young men and women, is the single acknowledgment by the Counsel that the Standard workers might return at night. In fact, Peter had passed by only a few minutes before, his double-barreled shotgun slung over his shoulder. He hadn't seen her, and Caleb had reacted with no more than a twitch of his ears.

She has just closed her eyes and is thinking that it is time to get in bed when Caleb's head lifts and turns toward the dirt road out of their valley. Mavis's hearing is acute, and within twenty seconds she makes out the low rumble of a truck. Her heart quickens as she gets up and vainly looks around for Peter.

Caleb jumps off the porch and trots toward the road. Mavis watches him for a moment and runs to the dining hall to ring the fire bell.

Her toe strikes a rock and she feels the pain. It barely breaks her stride, for she knows that the truck will arrive before anyone but Peter can respond to the alarm and her impetuous brother will endanger himself to defend the Glade. She reaches the pole that supports the bell and pulls the rope. Exposed for years to sun, rain, and winter, the rope breaks in her hands after one clap of the bell. She hesitates as the engine grows louder, not sure whether to run to the nearest cabin or go back to her own place for the rifle. There is no time. Gripping the rough pole hand and foot, she shimmies to the top and rings the bell. Splinters stab her palms as she slides down the pole. She drops the last five feet and runs back to the cabin to get the rifle that hangs over the door. By the time she gets there, the sound of the engine has stopped, and she sees the silhouette of the truck, barely two hundred yards away.

She pulls the rifle from its pegs, startled by the hollow explosion of Peter's shotgun. Not even checking to see if the rifle is loaded, she exits to the porch and sees two men, Hiram Brown and Dick McGee, running toward her. Two rifle shots shatter the stillness and she feels them in her own heart. By the time she reaches the path, there are several others closing on her. She hears her mother call "Mavis, wait!" Her mother's silhouette comes toward her and there are shouts and more shots, spattering and arhythmic.

"Stay back!" Mavis shouts as she runs toward the truck. Flames blossom from the roofs of the two cabins closest to the gate. She gets as close as she can, crouches, her rifle ready, but afraid to fire. In the confusion and darkness she can't see which of the moving shadows are the raiders. For the first time she checks and sees that the clip is loaded with bullets.

Shadows backlit by the quickening flames flee toward the truck, stopping to fire while others either pursue them or fall to the ground. A finger of fire rushes down the side of the Sayre cabin and Mavis realizes that the raiders have thrown gasoline on the houses. She gets up and runs toward the truck. Mavis stops within range, brings the rifle to her shoulder, aims at the truck and fires off three rounds as it begins to move. She knows it is futile, but it feels good to do something, and the kick of the rifle releases some of her tension. She fires a fourth round at someone being pulled over the tailgate of the truck. The truck retreats and her eye shifts to the cabins already wrapped in wild, yellow flame.

She realizes that her mother is beside her, and together they rush toward the burning cabins. People are running here and there in the palpating light of the fires, but it is too late to do anything. Sarah Sayre is standing as close as she can to the pyre that has been her cabin, a cracked blue teapot clutched in her hands.

Leah puts her arm around the woman and Sarah says in a flat voice, "Cy saved mother's quilt."

Both Mavis and Leah look anxiously at everyone who pass by. No one seems to notice them until Thule approaches looking grave and apologetic. At the sight of him foreboding makes Mavis shiver. Leah stares at him for a moment before she says, "It's Peter isn't it?" He nods, his face rigid and sober.

"Is he hurt bad?"

"He's gone, Leah."

"Take me to him," she says, her voice quiet and restrained. Mavis draws closer to her mother, takes her by the hand, and the two women follow Thule toward the place where the truck has been. Mavis holds the tears back. Beside her, Leah is quiet, still unbent, yet her eyes seem to focus on something beyond her sight. Peter is lying in the grass on his back, arms and legs twisted carelessly, a look of surprise locked on his face. Leah stares down at him and without turning to her daughter she says quietly, "Let's take him home."

"I'll help," says Thule.

"We'll manage. I've carried him before. This'll be the last time."

"Mother," says Mavis but before she can stop her, Leah stoops and tries to pick Peter up. She manages to lift his shoulders before she collapses beside him.

THE SIXTH DAY

—1—

The next morning, if morning is possible in a windowless underground room, is as despondent and heavy as the air. Bran, Ephus, and June are confined to Nikanor's office and the room across the hall. They have slept there "for their own benefit," as Nikanor put it, for the less they knew about Unity America the better. Nikanor came and went but he tries to relieve their suspense with distractions. Someone brought them a tape deck and a dozen tapes, a Monopoly set, and a deck of cards but nothing helped. Ephus worked a few wooden puzzles but was restless as a caged fox and he complained of a headache from the "dead air." Outwardly calm, Bran says little and June is alternatively thoughtful, restive, and morose.

Despite Bran's gloomy preoccupation, he forces himself to be interested in a book filled with pictures of stone churches resembling sculpted rocks, their spires pointing to something invisible in the sky, their brilliant windows brighter than any field of summer flowers. Another has pictures of paintings, views of serene well-fed people enjoying a picnic under a tree or rowing down a green river, living a life that seemed free of the hardship and privation that he has observed. Did this world exist alongside the one he knows, just as the walled villages exist within sight of the *Sal Si Puedes*? Is it gone or did it ever exist? He would ask Nikanor.

Nikanor joins them for lunch, a bar of chocolate and a bottle of wine in one hand and a thick file in the other. He is friendly but seems preoccupied with his work for his eye keeps drifting to the closed file as though he should be studying it. Bran notices that it is labeled "Standard–Ref–I–Security". He shows Nikanor the pictures in the book and Nikanor tells him that they are paintings by artists done over 100 years ago.

"Are there still places like that?"

"Maybe. Things keep changing."

Bran looks at the photos on the wall and asks him about the two men. Nikanor stares at them with respect and tells him that they are Thomas Jefferson and Martin Luther King. He takes a bite of his peanut butter sandwich, gets up and goes to the shelves, finds two books and hands them to Bran.

"Why are their pictures on your wall? Are they important to your organization?"

"They are both Americans who lived in different times before the Dissolution. Yet they shared a common vision," says Nikanor, his voice somehow changing, as though the words have come from a deep source of conviction.

"Why did the United States break up?"

Nikanor's eyes turn toward Bran with gentle indulgence. "The leaders lost faith in the vision." He stares at Bran, waiting for a response. Suddenly, as if an alarm has gone off in his head, he gets up, grabs the file and says in his usual bright tone, "Gotta go to a meeting."

Mid-afternoon, someone brings a pot of herb tea and slabs of ginger cake. They eat for the most part in silence. Having pinched the last morsel of the sticky cake between thumb and forefinger and licking them clean, Bran looks at June, her head bent over a magazine and says, "You've been staring at that page, the whole time you've been eating the cake." She looks up with a sad acknowledgement but says nothing. It is not like Bran to pry into other people's troubles, but perhaps to relieve himself of his own preoccupations or to cheer June up, he says, "You'll get out of here pretty soon, after Nikanor fixes you up with some fake identity papers like he promised."

"Hmm."

"What do you think you'll do?"

"I'll...probably try to leave California. Go east."

"Why east?"

June looks up at him, a bitter hopeless look that is both a tight smile and a frown. "I don't know," she says hanging on to the last word with a kind of desperation. "I don't know."

"It's not easy," says Bran trying to console her.

June looks at him with a beguiling sadness. "I've been thinking that I would have been better off back at the Institute. At least I belonged there." Her voice breaks and she pauses, "At least I had an illusion of pride."

He walks closer wanting to say something kind. "You're great; a hero inside and beautiful outside." June touches his arm with the tips of her slender fingers. Her eyes brighten with held-back tears. "If you've got no place to go, you can come back with me to the Glade. It's a quiet life. You won't feel mocked there." He says this knowing that it probably wasn't true. He looks at her through the mist of his thought and sees her sad smile of understanding.

Suddenly Ephus says, "There's worse off," and he glares at nothing in particular.

"You're right, Ephus," says June, and for the first time since they had freed her, she begins to display her usual self-possession. She twists a lock of her hair and says, "Maybe I'll find some people who are like me in Los Angeles."

Bran returns to the armchair and browses through the books Nikanor has given him. An hour passes in the stuffy room, an hour in which he does his best to amuse Ephus with arm wrestling, reading, riddles, anything he can think up to keep the boy from running off down the hall and trying to find the open air.

They are in their thirteenth game of tick-tack-toe, when Nikanor comes into the room with his sober blue eyes fixed on Bran. "That policeman you brained is dead. So the police want you back." The bottom went out of his stomach as Bran hears this, his revulsion at having killed a man mixing with the fear that he would be hunted forever. Nikanor touches him on the shoulder. "I know how you feel. I've been there too." Bran stares at him, his features contracted. Nikanor's hand massages his back, then he lets his hand drop and he turns toward the door as though he has remembered something. "At least you won't have to worry about the police. We can fix that up." Bran stares at his broad back and wonders how.

Each time Nikanor returns to his office, Bran looks up expectantly but the best that he gets in return is a sympathetic smile, or a "nothing yet." After dinner Nikanor comes into the room, takes out his violin and begins to tune it. He looks at Bran; sees him staring at the book but not really seeing it. June is running a comb through her hair, looking at the wall as though something is written on it. Ephus is playing with the first manufactured toys he's ever seen; a set of plastic building materials with fasteners and he is building a tower that is already two feet high. "Worrying about the money, I guess?" asks Nikanor.

"That and jail. What are my chances of staying out?"

"If you go to trial you've got as much chance as a steer at a slaughter house."

Bran takes a deep breath. "How long?" he could hardly say the words.

"Twenty-five years. Five years for killing the policemen and twenty for saving my life."

"They must want you as bad as a rogue bear."

"They keep tryin'. If you turned me in they'd gladly give you your $20,000 Old Dollars and then some," Nikanor says, with a wide grin. He touches Bran on the shoulder. "Don't worry about jail. Tomorrow morning you'll have identity papers and even work permits. All you have to do is grow a moustache and you'll be as safe as I am."

"That's what I'm afraid of, Nikanor. I don't want to live the life of a fugitive, running from the police. I want to go back to the Glade."

"Bran, you're an outlaw. That means they don't have any information on you in their data bank. And for a thousand dollars, which we will pay, a clerk will lose your file at the Court House. For the time being though your description will be on all the computer terminals of the inspection stations. You'll just have to avoid them when you can." Nikanor finishes tuning his violin and plays sonatas that are alternately happy and sad. He is in the middle of a soaring cadenza when the door opens and a stocky man with a swarthy complexion comes into the room. Nikanor stops. Still holding the instrument to his chin, he asks, "What's up Georgiu?"

"We found him, we think." Bran's head snaps up.

"Is he here?" Nikanor asked.

"Not yet but soon. They pick him up at bus station."

Bran jumps out of his chair, lets out a yelp, and claps Nikanor on the back.

"Don't get your hopes too high, it could be a mistake," says Nikanor. Bran walks around the room tormented by the thought that Jonah has squandered the money. He drops back into his chair and tries to think about Mavis. He remembers the deep-breathing exercises and begins them. His mind focuses on the stream that runs through the Glade and he grows calm.

"Here he is, Bran, the poor man has the flu," says Nikanor. Jonah, faltering and bent, shuffles into the room and falls into a chair. Jonah is empty handed and Bran's heart rises up into his throat. No pack, no money, he assumes, until his hope breaks through and he reasons that Jonah must know where most of it is. If he is sick he couldn't have spent it. He still has it, he concludes, and resolves to make Jonah tell him. Bran looks across the room at June. There is a mad light in her eyes that reminds him of the luminosity before a thunderstorm, and yet her face yields no other hint of emotion. His gaze returns to Jonah. Pathetic as he appears, he arouses only Bran's disgust. Jonah stares up at him, his eyes wide and fearful, and he seems to recoil to imaginary blows.

Nikanor slips out of the room for a moment and returns with a brown paper bag which he hands to Bran. The blood rises in his neck as he spills the contents out onto the table and begins to count the money.

"It's all there," says Jonah, his voice congested. Bran looks at him, and sees that he is shaking. He looks down at the money as Jonah explains that he had only taken the pack to safeguard it when Bran had been taken by the police. He came down with the flu and had been too sick to return it.

"What were you doing at the bus station then?" asks Nikanor.

Bran looks up from the counting, feeling his whole body drop with relief. "It's all there, all but twenty New Dollars."

"I borrowed that for the hotel and food."

Bran puts the money back into the bag. He walks closer to Jonah and sees that his forehead is beaded with sweat and tremors are passing through him like electricity. As he looks at the old man, pathetic and cowering, waiting for the expected blow, he realizes that he wants to believe Jonah's story. Jonah is pathetic, like so many other old husks he'd seen on the streets. He needs to focus his anger on the police who have tortured him, who wanted to shoot Nikanor, on the people who wanted the Glade, on the man with the pistol who robbed victims of an accident, on all the anonymous sources of cruelty. Jonah is only one of the victims; adrift, devious when he needed to be to survive, but not lacking in kindness. He feels contempt for him but he can't hate him. Bran suddenly feels very weary, and he shrugs, turns away, and sits down.

"Do you want him for anything more?" asks Nikanor. Bran looks up at him and he sees respect in Nikanor's eyes.

"No. Take him back to the bus station. The money's all I wanted."

Nikanor turns and explains to Jonah, that if he says anything to anyone about what has happened or where he has been, they will find him again and make him sorry. Jonah watches him as he might look at a poisonous snake.

"Can I go?" he asks, his voice rising.

"Yes,"

A wild look of relief in his eyes, Jonah stands. He is halfway to the door when June intercepts him and with such speed that no one could have stopped her, she raises her right arm and chops Jonah across the bridge of his nose with the edge of her hand. A strangled scream gurgles out of him as the cartilage cracks, he wraps his hands across his face but the blood gushes through his fingers and runs down his wrist to the floor like dripping red paint. June doesn't even look to see what she has done. She wheels and walks back to the table with the appearance of serenity and innocence.

"Better take him to the infirmary and stop the bleeding before you take him back," says Nikanor to Georgiu. Bran looks at him and sees a gleam of bemusement in his expression.

Held up by Georgiu, Jonah shuffles down the hall, moaning to himself.

Nikanor walks to the table and reaches into a drawer for a white rag. "I'll do it," says June, taking the rag from him, and walking over to the door she slowly mops the spotted pattern of blood off the concrete.

"What did you do that for?" asks Bran.

Without looking up, and still rubbing the residual stain she says in a gentle, tired voice, "For everybody."

Nikanor snorts and looks at her with eyes that are both gentle and grim. Then he walks to the table and says to Bran, "I've got your new identity here, you can become a farmer again."

Bran examines the card with the name Brandon Hawley and his picture. "Looks like I've had to become a fugitive to join society."

Nikanor looks at him, his expression impassive but with the cast of someone who has a minor ache. "I'm surprised you didn't do what June did."

"Giving him a split lip won't change anything."

"There's a thing called justice," says Nikanor. "Isn't that right, June?"

"Don't ask me. They never taught us about justice, only about right conduct."

"And what is that?"

"Honor, duty, loyalty; the qualities that bond one person to another."

"And what about the bond of people to society?" ask Nikanor.

June looks across the room at him with an earnest, level gaze. "Society is just an idea. It doesn't even exist."

"So how do you explain towns, cities, people who speak a common language, share common traditions?"

June looks at him steadily; she passes her hand over her mouth and says, "It doesn't make them any more understanding or willing to put themselves out for a total stranger. The only real bonds between people are personal." The words came out of her in a stream like an oft repeated prayer.

An indulgent smile opening his thick lips, Nikanor turns toward Bran. "What do you think?"

"All I think is that I'd better get back on the road before something else happens. What about you, Ephus?"

"Me too," says the boy looking up with adoring eyes at Bran.

"We've heard from the pragmatist," says Nikanor, then he goes on to say that it is too late to get a bus south tonight. Food is brought and as they eat, Nikanor talks about the American Revolution, a time when the settlers had taken up arms to get rid of a government that they didn't like. Bran has never heard of it but he rejoins that, "We are taught at the Glade that when you use violence, even for good purposes, you eventually become just like the people you're fighting."

"Sometimes it's the only way," says Nikanor.

Bran pushes his bowl aside, reaches for another slice of bread. "You're supposed to separate yourself from the evil until it passes, like getting in out of a snowstorm."

"What if it don't stop?" asks Ephus looking from one to the other.

"A rock endures frost and sun."

"I ain't no rock!" exclaims Ephus tearing into a piece of bread to prove it.

June smiles at the three of them, the first truly bright smile since her abduction, and she says, "Even a rock gets tired of enduring and turns to sand."

"You ever kill anybody?" Bran asks, looking at Nikanor.

Nikanor returns a hard smile. "We don't have to kill. Property is valued more than life, so we destroy property."

He has avoided the question, Bran thinks. Something Ragnar has said comes to him. When you save somebody's life you have a special bond to them. You're like a parent; you've brought them back into the world. He had saved Nikanor, and he didn't regret all the trouble it had caused him but he suddenly wanted to be done with the man, to get him out of his life.

"Will you get me and Ephus a ride to the bus early tomorrow morning?" he asks.

"We can all go together," says Nikanor. "I've got to go to Los Angeles. I'll be your guide."

"You already went to enough trouble. Just point us in the right direction. With the ID we'll make it," says Bran, fearful of more complications.

Brushing aside Bran's protest, Nikanor explains that the "buses won't be safe for you, what with the Inspection Stations."

"Then what good is this?" Bran asks, pulling the identity card out of his pocket.

"It'll work fine in a few months, but now it's chancy. Of course, the odds are in your favor if you want to risk it."

Bran stares at the pass, already resigned to accept Nikanor's notion of the best way to go. Nikanor explains that tomorrow at dawn they can all go together in a truck at least as far as the end of the Valley and from there they will have a little hike on the Thief's Highway.

"How long will it take to get to Los Angeles?" asks Bran, still skeptical.

"Two days," says Nikanor. "That's the safe way over the mountain trail. We could fake a long-distance police pass for you but you might not get any farther than the Fresno bus station."

They discuss the alternatives and Nikanor persuades both Bran and June that the safest way to travel is with him. He is road-wise and has contacts on the way.

"Now you'd better get a good night's sleep. Tomorrow will be a long day," says Nikanor. Bran watches him go, wondering what new trouble the man would bring him.

—3—

Having convinced Bran to go with him to Los Angeles, his mind bubbling with a new thought, Nikanor rushes down the corridor to Room H-2. Inside, he finds Betsy bent over a galley proof. She is the editor of Common Sense, the newspaper, and overseer of public communication for the Executive Committee. She looks up and her concentration shifts to welcome, glowing with some deeper feeling for him. She straightens in her chair, runs her hand over her slate grey sweater to smooth it and looks at Nikanor, her pale grey eyes deceptively innocent.

"Where's Tom?" Nikanor asks as he pours himself some tea.

"Recording his weekly panegyric to Democracy."

"He never seems to run out of words, but he repeats himself," says Nikanor, sitting down beside her and staring at the column.

"Don't we all?"

"What's the circulation of Common Sense now?"

"Sixty five thousand."

"We makin' any money?"

Betty's narrow lips pursed into a smirk, "We're being bought by the L.A. Times, hadn't you heard?"

"Nobody tells me nothin'."

She stares at him with that familiar starchy bemusement, and he thinks back on their long-ago not-exactly love. She had been the first woman after his wife's death. He had never loved her. His love was buried somewhere in the ashes of Detroit.

"They picked up that creep that stole Bran's money. It's all there." She looks confused at first, but she shares his satisfaction as a mother might indulge a child's anecdote.

"You'll be packing them off to the bus station tomorrow?"

"No, they're going with me to Los Angeles," he says, knowing that he has shocked her and steeling himself for the lecture that would surely follow.

"Cris, you are positively out of your mind!" she says, enunciating each word. "We've got a dangerous revolt that threatens to split the organization in two with one group going toward conventional terror. You're committed to the biggest, most difficult operation yet. Rudolfo Escamilla wants to kill you, not to mention everybody else, and you propose to wander off down the Yellow Brick Road with a bumpkin, a waif, and an incipient whore."

Nikanor listens, a broad smile pasted across his cheeks. He snorts several times as if to stop her, but she goes on finally winding down like a broken clock. "You done?" She is about to say more when he touches her lips with his fingers. "I've got it figured out, Betty." He took a deep breath. "I'm quietly pulling out of the San Pedro refinery operation." He watches the surprise register on her face. "Rudolfo wants the credit; he can have it and maybe get his head blown off in the process."

"You think it will fail despite all this planning?"

"It'll fail all right because a double agent will tip off Standard Security."

He waits for the expected reaction, a torrent of argument, but she says nothing. Her silence bothers Nikanor. There is a judgment in it. It is tantamount to killing Rudolfo and his radicals, but after all, they wanted to kill him. And if they weren't stopped, in their narrow impatience they would undermine everything he and the others have laboriously built. He has talked to people everywhere, and he is sure that the mainstream of Unity America, including most of the Hispanic members, are afraid of Rudolfo and the militants. "They want to play by their own rules; we'll help them." He pauses and she says nothing. Even her eyes are mute. "It's a no-lose case, Betty. The odds are that Rudolfo will fail, even get killed. We know how reckless he is. He'll be right up front. And we'll be rid of him. He'll be a safe martyr. And we can blame the militants for the failure. What do you think?"

"You've never done anything like this before, Cris. I know they're a crazy bunch of thugs, but to deliver them like packaged ham, knowing they'll be killed..."

"The end justifies the means."

"Does it?"

"You're the philosopher. You think about it. I'm going down the Valley over the Thieves' Highway tomorrow morning with my little gang."

"Sure you want to do this?"

"I've already put the bait on the hook. Rudolfo's our Benedict Arnold, Betty. He's our Benedict Arnold."

"It's your department. But do you still have to go?"

"I think so."

"Be careful," she mutters and goes back to her editing.

Nikanor leaves the room, brooding over the criticism. Too detached to be seduced by his own rationalizations, he knows that ten years ago he would have reacted differently. But principles, like tire treads, wear thin with use. No principle or rule applied when Unity is in danger of splitting up. Without the organization he might as well make a paper airplane out of his principles and try to fly it to the moon. He slams his fist into his hand, feels the sting radiate into his arm, and decides to play his violin for half an hour.

THE SEVENTH DAY

They are traveling along a two-lane asphalt road between fenced fields strung with grape vines, their broad leaves yellowing. Receding on the right is a small farmhouse, low and partially hidden behind tall trees, typical of the Free Agricultural Zone of family farms that surrounds the Free City of Fresno. Within twenty minutes the grape fields end, and they cross a stretch of vacant land, tufted by dry, wild grasses.

"We're coming to the Corporate Lands," says Nikanor. "Get your identity papers out. From here on down to the foot of the Valley we'll be traveling across land owned by the Standard Company."

"Those are the ones that want to open the mine," Bran says.

Nikanor turns in his seat and looks at Bran. "Are you all comfortable back there?" Bran, June, and Ephus are sitting on cushions on the floor of the van leaning against the sides. Signs beside the road tell them to stop for an agricultural inspection and within a few hundred yards they park beside an office painted red, white, and blue. Bran feels a ripple of apprehension and he looks at June seated across from him wearing her usual tight-fitting faded jeans and work shirt open to the top of her breasts. Her eyes, dull blue in the shade of the van, show no sign of concern; there is rather a look of enjoyment that reassures him. She looks toward the face of the inspector in the window of the driver's side with an inviting smile and casually pushes a skein of her hair up under her cap. The inspector, a man in a blue uniform with a red, white, and blue striped circle on his chest, meets June's eyes, responds with an admiring gaze and doesn't even look at Ephus and Bran. He glances at their documents, asks if they are carrying any produce, and waves them on.

As they drive away Nikanor says, "They don't have computers at stations like this so there's no risk unless you've got some kind of bugs or blight with you to kill the crops. Then you're in real trouble."

They ride between fields uniformly fenced with barbed wire, the rows of low crops, symmetrical, and stretching endlessly to low hills blurred by haze. Narrow paved roads divide the numbered fields and run off at right angles. Spurgeon, the driver of the van, explains that the roads go to villages where the employees live. With the austerity of the Glade in mind, Bran asks what they are like, and Spurgeon explains that they have, "real nice houses, schools for the children, swimming pools, and a club house. Standard takes good care of its people." He goes on to talk about the hard life of the independent farmers who have to sell their raisins to Standard at whatever Standard pays, or ship their crops by short-haul trucks down to Los Angeles, where the brokers take advantage of them.

Bran gazes at the precise rows and wonders how they have come to be so perfect. Despite his misgivings, he is beginning to think that traveling with Nikanor is the surest way to reach his destination. Other than the one they have just passed, there isn't a single inspection between Fresno and

Los Angeles on the route they are taking. Although it is much slower, he will have a much better chance of getting there. He feels the money secure in a money-belt and takes a deep breath of the air blowing through the window, dry and dusty, but better than the closeness of the jail and Nikanor's office. It is all working out.

The van stops next to an old elm, which provides shade for a single, green picnic bench. A sign proclaims that the rest area, complete with toilets, is a service of The Standard Company. Overhead, the sun and a convoy of dense cumulus clouds are playing hide and seek. Sprawled against the fence in the dry grass, they eat bread and string cheese.

They travel on through orchards of fruit and nut trees, each the exact same height, perfectly spaced, running for miles over otherwise barren ground. As they near the end of the Valley, the dark brown features of the high hills rise above them and they turn right on a smaller road toward the descending sun and a lower line of undulant hills. The sun is breaking like an egg-yoke on the edge of the hills as Spurgeon again stops the van. The fences that have followed them all afternoon end a half mile distant where the hills begin their rise.

"End of the line," says Nikanor, reaching behind him for his pack and violin case. "We walk the ridge trail from here and Spurgeon goes on to a ranch in the hills." They get out and watch as the truck moves down the road. Bran stretches and hoists his pack, looking forward to a hike after a day bouncing in the van.

"Take off your pack, there's no hurry," says Nikanor. He looks around and lets his eyes rest on a square concrete building standing about a hundred yards inside the fence in a field of cauliflower. "We haven't far to go tonight. Just look at that sky!"

Bran and June exchange impatient looks. "We're better off walking with the remaining light," says Bran, but Nikanor is gazing at the flattened sun on the rim of the hills. The chill is growing and the air is pungent with the smell of grasses growing on the hills. Overhead the bellies of the clouds are turning a salmon color while their bodies are deepening steel grey in contrast with the pale blue-green of the sky. Bran looks from the precise endless rows toward the rough hills.

Nikanor stretches out in the grass with his hands behind his head. He looks up at Bran standing over him and finally says, "We've got to wait until dark."

"Why?"

"It'll be safer. I'm going to blow up that pump house."

June gives him a wry look; she shakes her head and turns away. Bran feels his temper rising. Why did Nikanor have to expose them to danger? "Can't you leave well enough alone? I've had a whole day now without getting robbed or hit on the head. Why spoil it."

"Standard's your enemy too, Bran. They're the ones that want to steal your land, and Standard is the only barrier that stands in the way of restoring democratic government here in California"

"So do you think that if you blow up that pump and ruin all those crops they're just going to throw in the towel and give up?"

"Step by step, Bran."

"That government that you keep talking about got us to where we are today."

Nikanor sat up. "We can talk about that later. Right now, I'm going to wait until it gets dark enough that people won't see us cutting that fence and climbing into the building."

"Leave me out of it," says Bran widening his stance as if he were expecting to be shoved. "One time in jail is enough for me."

"Look around you," says Nikanor, "There's about as much risk as falling out of a sleeping bag."

"Depends on where you happen to be sleeping," says June who looks like she is enjoying the argument.

"Just walk on down the road, Bran, and take the first trail on the left if you're afraid," says Nikanor. "Wait for us at the top of the ridge."

"I'm not afraid! I just think it doesn't make sense; even if you happen to be right."

The light bleeds out of the sky and the clouds became more and more like smoke from a distant fire. Bran takes a few steps toward the hills and turns back. They might need him but it will be the last time he would be drawn into Nikanor's war with Standard. It is not his way and never would be. He looks at the planted fields, long stripes running to the end of his vision. Whatever the grievance, it is wrong to destroy life and wrong to destroy growing food.

"It's dark enough to begin," says Nikanor. He removes a wire-cutter from his pack, cuts an opening in the bottom of the fence and slides under. "Somebody pass me my pack and violin case," he says and Ephus complies.

"Do you intend to fiddle while the pump house burns, like Nero?" asks June.

"I keep the explosives in the violin case." Nikanor walks toward the pump house saying over his shoulder, "I could use a little help."

"I'm already a fugitive." says Bran.

"Oh, stop quibbling!" says June already moving toward the gap in the fence. "Let's just help him and get away from here." Bran watches her and, feeling embarrassed , he follows.

Nikanor circles the building, noting the steel door and a single narrow windowless opening about eight feet up one side of a wall. He pulls a flashlight out of his pack and illuminates the window.

"There's a wire screen. June, you're the lightest. Get up on my shoulders," He bends down to his pack, retrieves the wire-cutters, and hands her the flashlight and the tool. "Get up there and cut the screen away." June climbs from his hand to his shoulders and laboriously cuts the wire mesh. She describes the machinery to Nikanor, and he lowers her to the ground.

"Ephus, you're the only one who can get through that hole to place the charge exactly where it will destroy the pump. Will you do that for me?"

"Yup"

"Nikanor, you must be crazy. He doesn't know how to handle explosives. What if he drops it or jiggles a wire. He'll blow himself up and us too. Don't you care?" Bran says, concerned as much for Ephus as for himself.

"It's as safe as handling mud,"

"I ain't afraid, Bran," rejoins Ephus with scorn in his voice.

Nikanor assembles his bomb, sets the timer, and connects the wires. "This will go off in half an hour. We'll have plenty of time."

"Did you hear something?" whispers June.

"What are you whispering for? We sat by the road while the sun went down and didn't see a single car."

"Turn off the flashlight. There's one coming now!" says Bran and they all drop to the ground. Bran watches as the headlights come up the road. "Do you think you triggered an alarm?" he asks. Nikanor doesn't answer. Bran feels the tension rise as the car comes abreast of them, and for a moment, he even thinks that it is slowing down. They wait until the car is a quarter of a mile away. Nikanor produces a rope; he lifts Ephus on to his shoulders and the boy lets himself down inside the building. Within a minute he is back up and out.

"Couldn't have done it without your help," says Nikanor as he bends to stuff the rope and wire-cutters back into his pack. They have covered half the distance to the fence when they are knocked to the ground by the force of an explosion. Nikanor is the first to get up. "Let's go. The damned timer was defective."

Deafened, Bran doesn't hear him. He picks himself up and sees that June and Ephus are getting up as well. When they reach the fence Nikanor says, "That's never happened before."

"Always a first time," says June panting a little. Bran sees that Ephus is thrilled.

"What a bang!" the boy exclaims.

"You think anybody heard that?" asks Bran.

"I'm not waiting around to find out," Nikanor replies as he slips under the fence and breaks into a run down the side of the highway. At the end of the fence line Nikanor crosses the road and climbs a trail into the hills. They continue at a slower pace up a steep, but well- worn, path to the crest. Single file, buffeted by a chill wind, they walk the ridge, before descending into a pocket surrounded on three sides by steep walls. Nikanor drops his pack under a rock overhang. The air is still and the ground is dust-dry, indicating that they could sleep there even in the rain. Nikanor makes a fire; they eat their bread and cheese and feel the comfort of the fire's warmth and glow.

"Still mad?" asks Nikanor. Before Bran can answer, Nikanor pulls a bottle of brandy out of his pack and offers it to him.

Bran takes a sip, shakes his head and replies, "I know you're just doing the best you know how, like all of us."

"What's your California going to be like, Nikanor?" June asks, taking a sip and passing the bottle back to him.

"It won't be perfect, I can tell you that right now. But maybe, just maybe, it'll be better, for a while at least. Maybe people will respect each other more; not just because they are friends or relatives but just because they are people with common interests." Once started Nikanor's ideas pour out of him. Every person, Nikanor explains, is part of a great anonymous community in which each life is affected in a good or a bad way by what other people do. Bran appears to be listening but his eyes might have been glass.

Nikanor pauses and Bran looks at June the way one child would look at another child being lectured to by an adult. Seeing this she blurts out, "Nikanor, you can go on about that till dawn, but for me there is no more than the people I like and the ones I don't like, the one's that treat me kindly, and the ones that are nasty to me."

Nikanor growled his deep-down laugh and said, "I guess you two fit right in. I could just as well be talking to that rock." He looks over at Ephus, curled like a sleeping cat against the wall, and says, "Maybe Ephus has the right idea." Then he opens his pack and removes a faded brown wool muffler. He wraps it around his neck and settles into a niche in the wall next to Ephus. Nikanor's last words are, "Be sure you brush your teeth and turn out the light,"

June watches the shadows from the fire stroke Nikanor, then she turns toward Bran and says, "Walk with me a little before we go to sleep?"

He thinks about saying, there's no place to go until he remembers a small patch of dried grass perhaps fifty yards back, and he agrees. They walk single-file back to the level place that he remembered.

"Excuse me," says June and she walks away, drops her pants and relieves herself. June sits down beside him and they look up at the dome of the sky punctured by countless pins of light. "Know anything about the constellations?" asks Bran clasping his arms around his legs and pulling his knees up. "We used to make up our own stories-the shepherds."

"Weren't the myths good enough for you?"

"Maybe nobody remembered them."

"We studied them all," says June, leaning her shoulder against him and she points out a few obvious constellations.

"There's so much I don't know and never will," says Bran.

"You know what you need to know."

"I don't know that either," he says with a chuckle. "I used to think that I did."

They sit there for a time in silence as June's hand moves slowly to Bran's calf. Bran realizes why she has asked him to go with her. He welcomes her advances; it wasn't the same as infidelity. He is fond of her and he has to confess to himself that she is more than attractive. Her hand with its soft, sure, arousing touch moves toward his groin and she begins gently to fondle him. He doesn't hold back. June opens Bran's leather belt, the buttons of his pants, opening hers as well with the other hand, then slowly, she brings her mouth down on him and a thrill trembles through him.

He lays back, feeling like his bones have left his body. June takes his hand and guides it to her thighs. He opens his eyes to see June leaning over him, her face lit with quiet joy. June lies beside him for a time. She strokes his cheek and kisses him, her mouth pliant and yielding. Bran returns the kiss and they cling to each other, shutting out the night's cold indifference, shielding one another from the melancholy searching of the wind. Beside him, June dozes off, her head, cushioned by its soft hair, cradled on his arm. He thinks of Mavis alone, missing him, and he wonders what she would say if she could see him now.

THE EIGHTH DAY

—1—

A warming sun has the sky to itself. The wind has passed during the night and the dead grasses are yielding up a sweet scent of decay. Following the worn trail through the quilted grassland they join a rutted dirt track. It is the Thieves' Highway, the only road connecting the north and the south that is entirely free of inspection stations. On this route, fugitives, smugglers, thieves, transporters of marijuana, those with a reason to avoid the scrutiny of the authorities, are safe.

By mid- day, the fickle weather has turned. Heavy grey clouds threaten to choke the sky, their grey bellies tainting the hills, and the air is chill and damp. They get a lift in the back of a pick- up truck. A weary rain falls and the truck whines along in low gear, bouncing and sliding on the grades as they huddle against the cab. Bran takes Ephus under his poncho and June produces a yellow nylon slicker, while Niknaor sits in his heavy dark coat, the water beading on his ebony face.

Outwardly stolid, Nikanor is seething with thoughts. Committed to his intention of pulling out of the raid on the Standard refinery, he is thinking about ways of ensuring that the Militants don't become suspicious and back out. The security guard, Evers, should have alerted Standard by now. Nikanor has personally made a coded telephone call. That should work unless the Militants discover what he has done or why. Evers is no more than a paid informant who has initially been bribed to give Nikanor details of the refinery's security. Rudolfo's thugs are capable of beating the truth out of him and it wouldn't take much. He would confess that Fresno Unity has instructed him to betray them. He tries to put himself in the place of Deeters, the head of Standard Security. Given the information, he has no choice but to trap and kill the raiders before they do any damage. Deeters is the last person in the world he wanted to help, given his role in crushing the Detroit Free City. But why not use an enemy to destroy another enemy?

Beyond the raid, Nikanor has the lives of a few of his most loyal members to worry about and the delicate task of getting them out of the raid without telling them that it is a trap. And he must save his own neck, for he doesn't doubt the rumor that his own life is threatened by the Militants. He has never trusted Rudolfo Escamilla. People like Rudolfo acted out of rage rather than well-grounded belief.

But if Nikanor has learned anything since the Detroit uprising it is to trust no one and to assume that any imagined threat is real and must be dealt with as though life depended on it. That principle, applied without exception and combined with luck, has gotten him through the last sixteen years. He looks down at his violin case and wonders whether it might be leaking. It is time for a new one, he thinks, as he tucks it under his knees. Nikanor stares at his companions. Neither Bran nor June would ever become involved in Unity America. If Bran hadn't spent two days with Nikanor he would never have risked his life to save him. And yet if he had to pick someone to have as a friend it would be June, for loyalty is second nature to her. And it would also be Bran, for he did what he set out to do. It is all a matter of education. People are like bottles to be filled with good or bad water, although admittedly some of the bottles leak and can't hold anything and some are dirty and corrupted.

June finds herself looking again and again at Bran and thinking of the night before. Her insides feel like they are being stroked by something as light and ephemeral as a hummingbird's wings. She is feeling right about everything. She doesn't mind the rain and the chill, in fact she likes them; they are a part of the freedom that she has longed for and now has. True, back at the Institute she would probably be sitting in her warm room wearing something comfortable, reading a book, watching the rain from the inside. Here she can taste it, feel its chill, its sting, and for the first time she feels something profound and thrilling, as different as being in the rain is from looking out the window at it. She knows that her freedom is a part of it; she is free to grow, to experience whatever she chooses. And in a way Bran is a part of it, his rough good looks, the solid shape of him, the stolidity of his character, the dark moods always swept aside by his basic simple trust and good will. She looks at him, catches his eye, and pulls a little smile out of him. Looking at him makes her feel warm inside, makes her want to touch him, to be touched by him, be close to him. And as for last night, it has been like soaring and falling at the same time.

Bran sits on the damp seat of the truck bed feeling the chill of early California winter reach up his spine. He can only think about how slowly they are moving. He is so close now to his destination, and it seems past danger, but at this rate he could be too late. He thinks back on the circumstances that have brought him to this slippery mountain trail, but he puts the thoughts out of his head; as Ragnar has said, nothing came of pining for what might have been.

They ascend a rise, reach a rolling plateau and soon come to a crossroad, a dirt track passing into the wrinkle of two hills. The truck stops and the driver tells them that he is going west to Santa Barbara. They walk on, a fine rain falling like a mist out of nowhere, passing low houses of unpainted wood, small farms with gardens, fenced and furrowed with winter vegetables. On a hill near the road is a tall cross and Nikanor explains that a renegade sect practices crucifixion once a year at this place. "The Thieves' Highway is the only place where they can do it without police interference. Taking a life, even for religious purposes, is against the law in California Republic."

Late in the afternoon, with darkness settling early, they reach the top of a hill and see, halfway down the slope, a one story pitched-roof building, its unpainted walls faded to a silver grey. Several pick-up trucks are parked beside it, and a mottled horse is tethered in front of the wide porch.

"That's the Midway Inn. We'll spend the night there and we'll be in Los Angeles tomorrow."

"Not if we have to walk," says Bran.

"We won't. I recognize one of the trucks. He'll take us."

With its three small windows and low wooden ceiling, the public room of the Midway Inn is in twilight. A single pot-bellied stove takes the chill off the air. As Nikanor enters, his eyes dart quickly across the dozen road-weary men seated on benches at rectangular tables covered with red oil cloth. Bran relaxes as he feels the warmth and inhales the smell of soup cooked with meat and the damp sweat smell of clothing mingling with the resinous scent of marijuana smoke. Across the room, seated on an oversized arm-chair is a stout woman in her mid-sixties. Her face, like everything else about her, droops like melted candle wax but her small brown eyes, lively and alert, peer out of the sagging flesh as a child's eyes might be seen peeking through the slots of a witch's Halloween mask. They cross the room and stop in front of her.

Speaking in a low voice as if she didn't want to be overheard, she says, "What brings you up here on a wet day like this? Somebody tell you I fixed some rabbit stew?"

"You guessed it," says Nikanor with a broad, toothy smile.

They sit down at the table and Nikanor introduces each of them. The woman is called Mary Freitche, although that isn't her real name. No one on the Thieve's Highway used their real name, Nikanor explains. The only other person at the table is a man whose flushed face and sodden faded blue eyes, half shut and dull, announce that he is drunk. Nikanor tells them that he will be their driver to Los Angeles. A younger apple-cheeked version of Mary brings them large, steaming mugs of herb tea, bread, and honey. Bran warms his hands on the mug and recalls the times that he has done the same thing in Leah's kitchen after a cold day chopping wood. He looks across at June, her cheeks glowing, her eyes childlike as she gazes around the room.

"Is everybody friendly tonight?" asks Nikanor, looking from Mary to Patrick, tomorrow's driver.

The man answers quietly and not with the thick tongue of a drunk, "The one in the corner with the crimson stocking cap; I wouldn't turn my back on him."

"Anything to tell me?" "You might as well have it now as later," says Patrick, with the disembodied, precise speech that didn't seem to belong to his fog-shrouded eyes. "Sam Adams wanted you to know that Evers is missing. He doesn't know what happened to him."

Nikanor shakes his head. Now he can't be sure whether Standard Security knows of the raid. And even worse, Rudolfo and his thugs might know that the raid is to be a set-up.

"One thing more, Nikanor. Sam says to tell you to watch out for falling rocks on the road."

"Thanks," says Nikanor. It is the confirmation that the Militants will try to kill him. He looks at Bran and another plan begins to take shape in his mind.

The room glares with phosphorescence and there is a rattle of sheet metal followed by the vibrating roll of thunder. As if a sluice gate has opened, hail rattles on the roof like a fall of gravel and lashes the sides of the building. Someone puts more wood on the fire and the stove fights against the wind shaking the walls. Smoke backs down the chimney, mingles with the marijuana, and a fog settles over the tables, dispelled here and there by the flickering kerosene lamps.

Bran and June are sitting across from each other and the warm, trembling light from the kerosene lamp reflects gold in her hair. The rabbit stew is savory and reminds Bran of Leah's cooking. There is squaw bread as well and Bran likes it so much that he has Mary write down the recipe.

June grows animated after dinner and talks about what she might do when they finally reach Los Angeles. "You'll go back to your valley as soon as you get the papers, I guess," she says. He listens to the music of her voice and his desire stirs even in this crowded, smoky room. It is awkward and embarrassing, this attraction, and yet he yields to it knowing that it is transient, like the birds that stop in the Glade on their way to someplace else. Bran shares his feelings for her in his warm gaze. She shudders as if she has been overcome with an unpleasant thought and says, "Think of me some night up there in your warm little cabin, some night like this, or some night like last night."

The words seem to float and melt with her sentiment, and he feels awkward as he recalls their intimacy. "I'll probably be somewhere far away with some very rich gentleman; someone with a yacht big enough to have a dinner party."

"I hope you get what you want," he says, thinking that she wanted so much that is meaningless to him.

Bedding down at the Midway Inn is a matter of finding space on the floor. Mindful of the stranger with the red cap, Nikanor chooses a place against the opposite wall and Bran agrees to sleep beside him. To reach Nikanor the man would have to cross the room in the dark, navigating around several sleeping men, and bend over Bran. The storm has subsided as they lay down but rain is still drumming steadily on the window. Soothed by the sound, tired from the all-day walk, Bran falls asleep at once.

—2—

Bran awakes suddenly with the sense that something is wrong. Nikanor isn't beside him. He looks around as best he can in the dark room but there is no sign that anyone else is awake. Had anyone threatened Nikanor he surely would have heard it. Then he sees a faint line of light from the kitchen. By then he is wide awake, conscious of the hard wood floor.

He must have slept on his shoulder for it is aching. The line of light in the kitchen door moves. Careful not to wake June who is sleeping beside him, Bran gets up and goes to the kitchen. Nikanor is sitting at the table hunched over a cup of tea in the light of a single guttering candle. The board under Bran's right foot squeaks and Nikanor jumps up, a knife brandished in his right hand. He is poised to attack and his blue eyes are cold as mountain granite in winter. At the sight of Bran the mood fades into fatigue and relief.

"I woke up and you were gone."

"Thanks for caring." Nikanor sits down and offers Bran some lukewarm tea. "I must have been bothered by that man on the other side of the room."

"Is it just the police that want to get you, Nikanor, or are there others?"

"There's your friends, Standard. And now some former friends down in Los Angeles," he says, his voice muffled and weary.

"Have they ever come close?"

"So far so good. But it wears you down, having to always expect that one day, when you have your guard down, your luck will play out." He takes a sip of tea and searches the shadows of the room as if he half expects to see movement. "You can't live your life in fear. You have to just go on about your business. There are plenty of hazards in life; disease, accidents. Even if we're lucky, sooner or later we all die of something."

At that moment Bran pities Nikanor; always running, scheming for what seems like a hopeless goal. "Do you have some family that you can go back to when you need a rest?"

"I used to. But they're gone. My wife, my kid; he would've been about your age, are both dead." Nikanor falls silent, and after a time Bran starts to get up. "I didn't mean to drive you away with gloomy, middle-of-the-night thoughts. Stay, if you can't sleep. I'm glad of your company."

"What happened to your family?"

"After the Dissolution, a mostly Black government took over the Free City of Detroit. They opened some plants and the workers ran them. The owners had a share too. After a few years the owners decided to take them back. They put together a private army and attacked the City." Nikanor stares at Bran as if he isn't sure how much he would understand. "I was on the Governing Counsel of the City at the time. We armed the factory workers and anybody else who was willing to fight. There were weapons in the National Armory. They surrounded the City and tried to starve us out." Nikanor warms to the story and with more ease, he talks, with increasing detail, about battles at plants, and eventually in the public buildings as more and more of the City fell into the hands of the mercenaries. "I was one of about fifty who escaped pledging to start Unity America, after the food, the ammo, and the hope ran out."

"That's when you lost your family."

"Before that; they were taken hostage. They, the mercenaries knew who they were. They killed them when we didn't surrender." Nikanor drops his heavy eyelids and stares at Bran, "Now you know a little more about me."

"Maybe I should try to get some sleep."

"Bran, I think you'll be relieved to know that I'm going to get you a ride right to the door of that office where you can get your papers. Then I think I can get you home quicker than you came. You'll need to let your people know you have the patent before Standard throws them out." Nikanor looks at him, his eyes conveying both a plea and command. "But I want something from you in return. You game?" Bran assents reluctantly feeling wary and suspicious. "I want you to deliver a message from me to somebody. It'll take an hour. You can do it after you come back from Irvine, where you'll get the patent. Will you?"

"I guess so."

"You just guess you will? I need an answer."

"Sure."

Nikanor nodded two times. "Good. Let's get us some sleep in what's left of the night."

THE NINTH DAY

—1—

The storm has been the first heavy rain of the season and once again it seems to Bran that his way would be blocked, this time by nature. Early rains always loosened the dry banks of the roads and brought down mudslides. Patrick, the driver, is optimistic as he climbs into the truck cab. "We had a lot of little rains this month, so it shouldn't be too bad. But just in case, we've got picks and shovels." The narrow road is wet, rocky, and sloping in places. Although they travel very slowly, they make steady progress, at least until they see the slide that covers the road. Ankle deep in mud, they slice away at it for two hours. Loose rocks impacted in the mud have to be rolled over the side, but fortunately none is so big that it couldn't be moved. They are covered with mud and exhausted when at last the truck, precariously tilted, its four wheels spinning and side slipping, passes over it.

Patrick proves to be a skilled driver, careful and quick to deal with the rough, sloppy surface of the track that at times is barely wide enough for the truck. He has to be adept, for not only did he carry supplies for the farmers in the region of the Thieves' Highway, he often transported hundreds of thousands of dollars' worth of marijuana from Mendocino farms to Los Angeles where they were transshipped to the East Coast and even Europe. Except for the produce of the vast Standard farms, marijuana is the leading cash crop produced by California Republic, according to Nikanor, looking at the canvas-covered bales that shared the truck bed. It is also a source of income for Unity America, providing much of the money for the food and health care for the poor.

Despite his lack of sleep, Nikanor is in good spirits as he recognizes the last ridge before the San Fernando Valley. His plan still seems feasible despite the news of the disappearance of Evers, the Standard security guard. He just has to stay out of the way of Rudolfo's thugs until he has met with his own people, and let Deeters, head of Standard Security, know about the raid. He looks across the truck bed at Bran. Bran will be the perfect messenger. Since he knows no one in the organization and no one knows him, there will be no one to connect him to Standard's readiness for the raid on the refinery. He hopes that Deeters is clever enough to trap Rudolfo.

The road ahead is pitted but paved at the point that the truck begins its descent into the San Fernando Valley. Except for some towering white clouds, the sky is blue and the visibility sharp. "You've made it, Bran," says Nikanor. Bran looks from Nikanor to June. There is excitement in her eyes as she gazes down at the grid work of streets and buildings stretching to the foot of sharply rising, rough brown mountains. "So many houses," June exclaims.

Nikanor turns a sad face toward her and says, "Look closer and you'll see that it's a city of the dead." Most houses have been reduced to flat piles of rubble, while those few still standing are little more than roofless frames, stripped of doors, even siding. Some have collapsed like old, abandoned chicken coops. Lawns have reverted to tall, dry, clump grass. Running diagonally across the valley is a jagged fissure with one side ten feet higher than the other.

They come to a wide street broken by cracks and encounter storefronts, boarded up or windowless. Nikanor explains that the San Fernando Valley was hardest hit by the great earthquake. Nearly every house had become uninhabitable and water, sewer, and electric services were destroyed. For the most part, the survivors had abandoned the area. Those who stayed on soon left as the continuing aftershocks, nearly sixty in all, and the permanent lack of water, drove them away. Services were never restored, and the Valley became a source of increasingly scarce appliances and building materials. Scavengers regularly drove the streets in old trucks taking what they could.

"It's become a kind of resources mine," says Nikanor. "Someday, they'll probably strip it back to its natural state, and start all over again." They turn away and pass through a valley between low hills covered with derelict houses. After riding along a dry riverbed of channeled concrete, they have a view of high towers rising like geometric mountains, more it seems than Bran can count, and in the foreground, a sculptured maze of raised roads intertwined like a loosely tied knot.

Nikanor tells them that many of the buildings are still in use, particularly the first four stories, but the upper floors are bird roosts, unsafe and windowless. The area has the look of Fresno with cars, trucks, and stores. More than a million people still live in a band along the hills stretching from East Los Angeles to the Pacific Ocean. It is like an island, producing everything it needed, even cars and buses. Across the walled river they could see a make-shift shanty town, a patchwork of walls and windows, pieces of San Fernando Valley houses stitched and stapled together. Windows hang at odd angles and here and there a wall is composed of five or six doors side by side. They enter a well-paved street flanked with busy stores and streaming with cars and people on foot. Bright colors contrast with the faded skeletons of the Valley, turquoise, mustard, and flamingo. The signs are all in Spanish. They turn down a narrow street threading among tawny-skinned people with Indian features and dark hair, dressed for the most part in bright colors. Within a few minutes the truck stops at their destination, the two-story stucco facade of the Hostelo de San Carlos.

—2—

It has been a long meeting and Gus Deeters, Vice President of Security for California Standard, is eager to wind it up. A tall, athletic man in his early sixties, Gus keeps to his schedule, and Tuesday racket ball at the Long Beach Athletic Club is at hand. Years ago, he had resolved that his heavy athletic build would not turn to "booze and butter fat", and he devoted at least an hour a day to exercise, not only because he wanted to stay in shape. He liked the way he looked and believed that it was his responsibility to stay healthy to function best in his job. And it is a big job; security employed nearly as many people as production. It had to, since the Constitution of California Republic had made law enforcement on private property the responsibility of the owner.

He looks at the hands of the clock--he hated digital time--and says, with a disarming smile, "You know me, I'm a stickler for the schedule, so if there's any more to be said about item seven, you've got twenty minutes. For my money you can hang around all night if you need to put something together for tomorrow, but I self-destruct in 20 minutes." Suddenly he looks stern, the frown lines on his high forehead deepen, both the horizontal ones that cross from left to right and the two that seem to give rise to his strong broad-bridged nose. "Unity America so far has been, ah, about as effective as a gnat on the nose of Beauregard, my father's breeding bull. It's not because they don't have the will or the way. We know they've got enough explosives stashed to put Los Angeles on the moon." He stops and fingers the buttons of his blue pin-striped vest as if he were already taking it off. There is a moment of confusion in his grey eyes, as though he has lost his train of thought, then he continues. "It's, ah, because of you boys that all they can do is take out pumps, like the one they got last night, and an occasional power transmission tower, like the one they hit last week."

"Two weeks ago, Gus." says Roger Critch, a square jawed, balding man, one of four seated at the conference table that abutted Deeter's cherry-wood desk. "It was a booster station in the foothills, west of some town in the Forest Service land last week."

"Templeton," says Don Frachia, his round choir boy's eyes wearing their guise of innocence. Frachia is a martial arts instructor.

"Time flies when you're having fun, don't it now" says Deeters, and the beguiling smile returns with its rival set of facial creases. His administrative assistant, Don, and the three other Assistant Vice Presidents nod and smile with ironic condescension. They know the boss's habits and are in fact just as glad to be rid of him and get down to serious work. He could be overbearing and opinionated, and once he decided something it would take a ton of lignite to blow it out of his handsome, grey-haired skull.

"You believe the story about the refinery? Sounds like more bull shit just to get us riled up and nervous," says Deeters, scraping his file together, a sign that he is almost ready to leave. "Escamilla and the Militants have been threatening to hit the refinery for years."

Frachia looked across the desk at him. "But now we've confirmed that they have security info. They bribed one of our guards."

"How do you know?"

"Just luck. He started bragging to a friend about all the money he was winning at the track. We hot-boxed him and he obliged us with everything. He confessed to giving them plans of the parts of the refinery and information about guard shifts and numbers of men on the shifts," says Critch, pulling down the corners of his mouth.

"Anybody I know?" Deeters prided himself in knowing every man and woman by name.

"A guy named Evers."

"You've taken steps."

"We've changed everything we could; times of shift, things like that. But he's hurt security, there's no doubt of that."

"Do we know anything about his contact?" Deeters asks, his frown lines deepening and a flush growing on his cheeks.

Critch fingers his file. "A guy named Cris. A big black dude; somebody who would stand out in a crowd. Six feet tall, and blue eyes."

"Where is this Evers now? Can I talk to him?"

Frachia sniggered. "If you like scuba diving."

"I see," says Deeters, fingering the buttons on his vest. It is Detroit all over again. The description is of Ludel Reed and to Deeters, Unity America is one man; Ludel Reed. Deeters had first heard of Reed during the siege of the Free City of Detroit. As head of the Militia, Deeters had, as he liked to put it, "scattered the revolutionaries like cockroaches when the light goes on." But Reed and some others had slipped away, gone underground, and surfaced years later with Unity America. He had studied Unity, read its propaganda, thumbed through its newspapers. They liked to paint themselves as patriots, but he knew that all the talk about "democracy" was crap. "It's Reed," he said. "If he was handling this Evers contact himself, we've got to take the raid on the refinery seriously."

"We are taking it seriously," says Critch, working his j aw.

Deeters checks his watch. "Seems like you boys have it under control. I'll look for the report of your meeting tomorrow morning." Halfway out the door he turns. "If we're lucky, Reed will be right there directing traffic. Wouldn't I like to hang his head over my mantle."

THE TENTH DAY

—1—

Bran rises early, having slept well despite his nervous anticipation. He washes thoroughly, changes into fresh clothes, and shaves, all the while feeling the eagerness to get this last lap over with. He has a whole day to travel just 40 miles or so and, except for one inspection point, he'd been told that there is no danger. Nikanor has arranged a ride for him with a priest, a tall, hollow-cheeked man with timid brown eyes and a loose mouth that seems to have been made to hang open. Father Sebastian, the driver, calls Bran by his new name. He's in no hurry and urges Bran to finish his breakfast. Bran, running on a different clock, bolts down his bread and hustles out the door and into the courtyard.

The priest's car is pathetic, its paint faded and oxidized to the color of metal. The windshield is cracked, and the upholstery of the driver's seat is torn. The priest is observant enough to see Bran's doubt, and he says, "Don't worry it's never failed me yet." The car seems to run smoothly enough although the priest isn't a very confident driver and the car vibrates as though it has palsy when it starts. Their path is through narrow crowded streets that look like the *Sal si Puedes* but with a more distinctly Latin flavor, so much so that Bran finds it hard to accept that he is still in California. Although the priest hadn't mentioned it, he soon stops before a plain doorway with the explanation that he has to visit a sick parishioner. The visit extends to the limit of Bran's patience. He sits, nervously shifting on a wooden chair that is too small for him, providing a diversion for a child of six—a talkative boy with round, sober eyes and an inexhaustible supply of questions. An old woman, as wrinkled as she is stooped, offers him a cold drink, a sweet tasting liquid.

The priest returns, and they go back to the car only to find a flat tire. He mutters something to himself, wrestles the trunk open and removes a piece of rusted equipment that he optimistically describes as the "you know, jack." He hands it to Bran with the apology, "I have no luck with mechanical repairs." Bran plays around with the accordion mechanism concluding after a frustrating five minutes that it is broken. One of the bystanders tells him about a car repair shop around the corner, and he follows the man only to see a pair of legs protruding from under the front wheels of a faded green pick-up truck. The mechanic isn't very interested in dropping his work and helping but when Bran tells him that the car belongs to Father Sebastian, a fact confirmed by the bystander, he comes out from under the truck, rummages in the darkness of his garage, and produces a greasy pedestal jack that he loans to Bran for a $10 deposit. Bran jacks up the car, wrestles with the partly rounded lug bolts and replaces the flat tire with a bald spare, all the while wishing that his horse would somehow appear. He returns the jack and they get under way, to the assurances of the priest that they would arrive in plenty of time.

Bran silently curses Nikanor for complicating things. He would have done better with the bus, even if it did pass an inspection station. He tries to relax and look at the monotonous chain of towns, one after the other, each with their frustrating stop lights and slow traffic. At least it is a fine autumn day, he tells himself; the air is fresh and the view of the mountains rising abruptly is a promise to him that within a day he would be on his way home.

They pass a sign that says "Irvine 9 miles" then another announcing that an Agricultural Inspection Station is a half-mile distant. So close to his destination, Bran is caught up in a sudden fear that even with his documents he would be identified as the murderer of a policeman. It is an irrational fear, but he has no experience and has no way of knowing how much information they have beyond his description. They might even have his picture by now or his fingerprints on the screen. For once there is no Nikanor to guide him. He is on his own with this timid priest. Impulsively he says, "Can we go around the inspection station?"

The priest shoots him a worried look and asks, his voice already tightening, "You're not a fugitive or something like that, I hope?"

"No. I've got papers, see?" he says pulling them out of his pocket.

"Just last week another priest got caught at this station with a smuggler he'd given a ride to, and they confiscated his car. It's the law. The priest slows down and pulls off the road. "If you're in any trouble, you'll have to go on your own from here."

Bran tries to reassure him but the priest's uncertainty only fans his own doubts and he begins to think about avoiding the station altogether by simply climbing through the barbed wire fence next to the road and going around it. The priest likes this idea and even offers to wait for him down the road beyond the station. Bran is about to do this when they notice that there is no more traffic coming from Los Angeles.

They look at each other and the priest says, "Probably just an accident, or a convoy." Bran gets out of the car and looks down the road. Father Sebastian opens the window and repeats, "I'll wait about half mile down from the station." Bran stares down the road again and recognizes runners. The engine turns over but refuses to start. The priest gets out, lifts the hood, and begins poking the loose skein of wires, muttering to himself.

"Don't look at me, I can't even drive," says Bran, watching the oncoming runners. "Can you tell me how I get to that records office?"

"You just turn right on Esmeralda in the middle of the town and go three blocks. You can't miss it. But I'll take you there." The lead runners are approaching, their stride telling Bran that it is a long-distance race. Bran strips down to his white undershirt and loose-fitting white under shorts. He ties his shirt and pants around his waist. A group of six or seven run by sweating and looking like they are beginning to tire. He waits as a larger group converges.

"Don't wait for me." He elbows his way into the center of the pack and begins to jog.

The priest looks up and bangs his head on the edge of the hood, uttering an angry "Jesus, Mary and Joseph!"

—2—

Dressed in a grey pin stripe suit, his face altered by a narrow moustache and wide tinted glasses, Nikanor is sitting at a table in a well-appointed restaurant across from the recently reopened Los Angeles County Museum. He looks across Wilshire Boulevard at a group of school children walking up the steps toward the entrance and imagines his son and wife in front of the Detroit Art Museum. The image dissolves into sadness and he wonders when he has last visited a museum. For that matter when has he done anything that wasn't essential to his work or his health? A copy of the Times is folded in front of him and a half full cup of coffee.

A stout, balding man smoking a briar pipe comes in the door, sees Nikanor, and sits down across from him. The waitress recognizes him and brings coffee. John Dickenson owns a store down the block, and often has mid-morning coffee in the restaurant.

As if to confirm the purpose of the meeting, Nikanor pulls a catalogue out of a briefcase and opens it on the table between them. "How's business?" Nikanor asks.

"The competition is aggressive as usual, and getting worse," the man replies, tapping his pipe in the ash tray.

"I think it would be a good idea not to participate in the trade show in San Pedro," says Nikanor. "It's supposed to be this Friday isn't it? I would tell people to stay away. And you should tell Rudolfo that I found out about his plan and that's the reason I'm not coming."

Dickenson's frown raised welts on his thick-skinned brow. "That makes sense although there's a risk that they'll get all the business down here."

"I'll take that chance."

"When are you leaving?"

"Tomorrow, if I can get a flight to Reno."

"I'll make sure you get on the plane."

"You want to see the pictures of the new line?" Dickenson nodded and before Nikanor left they riffle through a dozen pages of a catalogue showing pictures of sport shirts.

Dickenson gets up and Nikanor says, "Give Rudolfo the message today, will you?" Nikanor watches the Chairman of the Los Angeles section of Unity America turn away. "Don't forget your pipe." Dickenson reaches out a pudgy hand and retrieves it.

"I always forget it. They know who it belongs to. The coffee's on me."

Across the street the doors of the Museum open and the children began to file in. On impulse Nikanor decides to join them.

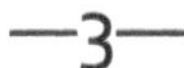

The inspection station is just ahead but Bran is confident that this many runners will simply pass through. Running as they are in shorts, there is nothing to inspect. And he is right, for the inspectors in their dark blue uniforms are simply standing by their booths watching like so many spectators. He simply jogs along in the herd, hidden under a blanket of sweat and the labored breathing of 200 runners. It seems so silly it makes him want to laugh. He is beginning to warm up, feeling his muscles loosen and already exhilaration is filling him with well-being. He has passed the last danger point. Now all he has to do is run another nine miles, easy for him, and hand over the money, tied securely around his waist.

Bran stays with the same group of runners for a mile or so then gradually, he begins to move forward, with the idea of making his own pace and leaving the race behind him. After all, who knew how many miles they have already run. He leaves the pack and begins to close on about 15 competitors scattered over the next half mile. In the next five miles he manages to pass all but four, three men and a woman, all with the lean musculature and steady gait of long-distance runners. They are the ones who have come to win, the ones to beat, and he watches as they take turns moving forward and pacing the others before falling back.

As Bran begins to close on them the lead runner, a tall man with tousled brown hair, looks back, and increases the pace. Bran whimsically thinks he might strive for the lead then decides against it. Nevertheless, he stays close to the pack, occasionally moving up when the pace slows, falling into the hypnotic rhythm, feeling both fatigue and well-being. It is early afternoon when they reach the outskirts of the town of Irvine. There is a surprising look of prosperity. The street is wide, lined with trees and the shops and apartment houses look well maintained. People are standing at the curb waiting, and he knows that the finish line is close.

The pack of leaders starts to run faster. Bran keeps up the pace and is the fourth to cross the finish line. A crowd gathers around the winner and the runner up, a woman with tousled hair. They are bent over, arm in arm, supporting each other and displaying weary victory smiles. A few of the people look up to watch Bran, but the admiration in their expressions turn to curiosity as he continues to run through the crowd.

Tired and thirsty, Bran stops at a service station to get a drink of water, ask directions, and put on his clothes. There is a map of the town in the office window. Esmeralda Street is six blocks ahead and it is only 3:00. He walks the rest of the distance chewing on a few dried apricots that he'd put into his pocket.

The brass sign in front of the circular stucco building reads, California Republic Central Land Registry, The Irvine Company.

The entrance is faced with two story glass windows and the floor in the lobby of the building is black polished marble, but Bran hardly notices. He finds the right office and approaches the counter, feeling a sudden choking apprehension that something would be wrong; they won't take his money or there is no record of their license.

A woman with a bland, wrinkled face and an orange head of hair frozen in waves looks up from the keyboard of a computer terminal waiting for him to speak. Bran explains his business, he hands her the original license to the Glade, and nervously waits as she studies it. She keys some numbers and information into the computer and waits as the machine chatters to itself. Bran has never paid much attention to computers although he'd seen one operate at the Forest Service Headquarters. He knows that they store information, and he watches the screen waiting for the answer to the woman's cryptic question. Some words and numbers dance across the screen, she digests the information, types something more, the machine chatters.

Still looking at the screen she tells him that the Standard Company has applied for the patent. "But you have the prior right if you can put up the fees." She looks at him skeptically. "They come to..." she looks back at the screen, "$188, 798. I'm afraid we would require cash or certified check as you probably know this is the last day before your priority expires." She stares at him, mild curiosity showing in her small, wrinkle rimmed eyes.

"Do I pay you?" asks Bran, fishing the wad of bills out of his pocket.

"What have you got there, Old Federal Reserve notes? I'll have to check the Treasurer's office to be sure we can take them."

"It's good money!" She raises her hand as if to calm him and smile, "I know that. It's just that you may have to take them to a bank and get them exchanged for New Dollars. You wait here." She disappears behind a partition. After a few long minutes she returns. "We can take the money." She sits down, punches her keys, and a machine spits out a document. He takes it down to the end of the counter thinking that he has out-maneuvered the defense and is about to put a good kick through the goal. The clerk at the cashier's window counts the money twice and punches information into another machine. She gives him another paper to take back to the other woman and some New Dollars. Without counting the money he returns to the other woman. She takes the papers, produces another one and says, "Here's your provisional patent. You'll get a permanent copy in the mail."

"What about the other application?"

She moves both of her hands in a horizontal gesture. "It's defeated. You hold the legal patent." He grins and reaches across to shake her hand. Suddenly he feels lightheaded, not sure whether he should collapse or jump up into the air.

The woman looks at him in a friendly way and says, "Now be sure you register that document in Templeton." He is about to leave when she adds, "And one thing more. Go across the hall and get yourself a Title Insurance Policy."

Bran is not sure what she is talking about, and she explains that if there is any trouble with Standard over the patent to the land, the Irvine Company would take care of it. Bran is skeptical but she reassures him that everyone does it, and since she seems to know what she is talking about, he obediently goes across the hall, applies for the policy and pays the $2,535 premium in New Dollars.

He leaves the building feeling expansive, finds the bus station and buys a ticket for an express to East Los Angeles. There is a lunch counter in the building, and he eats a ham sandwich before the bus loads. He buys a copy of a sports magazine to read on the bus. Bran boards the bus without fear. His success, the legitimization of the Glade's rights, his identity documents, all give him confidence and he even finds himself thinking how silly he has been to fear detection. Of course, he would have to pass through many inspections on the way home but he would risk it. He would even send copies of the documents by mail in case something happened to him, and he would travel the fastest route. No more hiking over Thieves Highway. That is even riskier. He looks forward to a long, slow week in which nothing unpredictable happens, and mostly he wants to be near Mavis.

He is in the middle of an article on Soccer when the bus begins to slow and he sees the red lights of the Inspection Station. For a moment he feels a twinge of fear, then it passes, and he goes back to his reading. He hardly glances at the inspector who looks from him to the picture on his identity card and hands it back. Bran looks up again to see the inspector moving back up the aisle with a man in front of him and he realizes that Nikanor has been right. It is best to stay away from them.

It is nearly 5:00 when he returns to the hostel to find June, Ephus, and Nikanor in the common room. Nikanor has blackened his hair and is wearing steel rimmed glasses. Dressed in jeans and a blue work shirt, he looks fifteen years younger.

"Just to look at you, I can see that you got your papers," Nikanor says. "The priest get you there in one piece?"

"Sort of." He fills them in on his day

"I'm going to Reno tomorrow morning, and I've got space for you and Ephus just like I said."

"What is it this time, mule train or a wheelbarrow?"

"A plane. It's the safest way. There are no inspection stations up in the sky."

Flying has to be dangerous Bran assumes, and there must be something that Nikanor is not saying. "What will the plane be transporting besides us, explosives?"

"Nothing like that. Not this time. I promise you."

Bran hesitates, weighing the risks. Ephus looks at him decisively and says, "I always wanted to fly ever since I saw a bird."

Nikanor says, his voice a little distant, "If you're lucky you could make it home on the buses in two days at most."

"C'mon Bran!" Ephus pleads. "I'm goin' even if you don't."

"What about that errand you want me to run for you, Nikanor? Is that part of it?"

"Yes, but there's no danger. It'll just take you an hour or so."

Bran stares at him skeptically. "Why don't you get one of your people to do it?"

"A TV camera takes a picture of everybody that comes through the door. They could trace one of our people. You are totally anonymous."

"I could do it," Ephus says.

"You ought to get back home quickly, Bran. No telling what Standard is up to now that the time has run out. They've probably got a bulldozer ready to flatten your cabins."

Again, Bran yields to Nikanor although he assumes that, as usual, there are unspoken risks both in delivering the message and in the flight. He agrees and Nikanor takes him to a quiet corner of the room before handing him the envelope with the name,

"Gus Deeters" printed on it, and a note showing the bus route to the building that houses the officers of the Standard Company.

"You want me to give the envelope to this man?"

"No, that would be dangerous for you, Bran. Just give it to the guard. The important thing is, nobody is to know where you are going."

"Sure."

Nikanor rewards him with a charming smile and a slap on the back. "Now go, before the buses stop running." He watches Bran go toward the door as a shepherd might watch his sheep dog. By now Dickenson would have gotten the message to Rudolfo, he thinks. Chances are the Militants didn't even know he is in Los Angeles. They knew he usually stayed at the hostel but they have never seen him so disguised. Besides, he intends to stay in his room until morning and the priests will warn him of anything suspicious. He thinks about the simple message and its effect on Deeters. "San Pedro raid, Friday. A friend." Maybe Deeters's ego will take him to the refinery to personally direct the defense. With fantastic luck Deeters and Rudolfo Escamilla will each get what they deserve. They certainly deserve each other; he says to himself as he climbs the stairs that lead to his small room.

—4—

Bran enters the lobby of the tall building branded with the now familiar red, white and blue circle. He gives the envelope to a guard behind a desk. "This is to be given to Mr. Deeters," he says. The building is clean and well maintained like the endless fields crossing the San Joaquin Valley. The guard is pleasant and polite. There is certainly nothing fearful about Standard. It is impersonal, but no more so than Unity America. He has to admit that all he knows about either Standard or Unity is what he sees; the people who work for it and what they do. Nikanor is Unity America; the guard in the lobby and the surveyors checking out the mine above the Glade are Standard. What they do make them good or bad, foolish or wise. He couldn't hate Standard any more than he could like Unity America. They weren't, after all, people, or the tree covered slopes sheltering his home. He rides the bus back to the Hostel, realizing that the torments of the past ten days are already turning to cartoon in his mind, events to be looked back on with the relief that they are past. He dozes off and nearly misses his stop. Back at the Hostel, Bran finds June and Ephus bent over a checkerboard.

"Where'd you go?" asks Ephus.

"I ran an errand for Nikanor."

June brushes a wave of her hair away from her broad cheek and glances at Bran, her eyes clouded with her unrevealed thoughts. "I taught Ephus checkers. He has a quick mind."

"She always beats me!"

"I'll get something to eat," Bran says, and he goes into the Dining Room. He eats quickly and returns to find them in the same place.

"I just jumped two of her pieces!" Ephus exclaims but his joy collapses as June jumps four of his and wins.

"You've got to look ahead in life, Ephus," says June, "Isn't that right, Bran?"

"As far as you can see."

A priest comes up to them. "Nikanor wants to know if your trip went as expected."

"Yes."

"He wants you to be ready to travel tomorrow at six." "I guess Nikanor must run this place too," says Bran. He sits down and, at Ephus's urging, plays a game of checkers with him.

"Will you take a walk with me?" June asks. He is tired and wants nothing more than sleep but knowing that it could be the last time he saw June, he agrees.

Rain has fallen briefly, and the street is awash with streaks of color from the garish signs and windows of cafes and bars. Prostitutes, male and female, are back on the street loitering in pairs in their tight body stockings; brazenly seducing passersby. Bran looks at them and is no longer shocked. He has come to accept them, as people accept everything after they get used to it.

A boy, scarcely in his teens, blocks their path. There is a moment of tension until he declares himself a seller of marijuana. A pair of drunks stagger by arm in arm, clutching paper bags in their free hands, their faces swollen and bruised. Bran looks at them feeling both sympathy and contempt.

"This is Hell," June says in a low, depressed voice.

"I'm glad I'm getting back to my garden." More and more Bran's mind, freed of its obsession, is returning to the ordinary details of his life. He visualizes the raised beds of the garden with its tall stalks of corn and cabbages. He wonders how the squash is doing.

"You could still come home with me, if you have a mind to." Bran offers that out of affection and loyalty, but he knows that June would have as much place at the Glade as a speckled trout in a mole hole. "We could use a good leather worker. You're pretty handy with that awl of yours."

"How would you know, you've only seen me use it as a dagger. Thanks, Bran. If I belong any place, it's here. Not on this side of Los Angeles, but the other side, where the rich people live."

"I guess I'll miss seeing that."

"I took a jitney ride up there to Beverly Hills today. It's the world I was prepared to live in; shops with expensive clothes, restaurants, clubs, nice looking people coming and going, shiny cars."

"Where do they get their money?"

"I suppose they buy and sell. Ask Nikanor."

"Thanks but I've heard enough of Nikanor's talk." They cross through an electric stream of song, harsh laughter, and stomping boots spilling out of the open door of a bar. A young man and woman in a doorway are wrapped around each other staring dreamily into each other's eyes. "You don't have to be rich to be happy."

"Are you happy?"

"Yes. I have everything I want."

"What's that?"

"A woman who loves me, who I love, other people who I care about, work that makes me content, things I like to do and do well, a place to live that suits me."

"You know what you want out of life."

"Being away helps you appreciate what you have." Bran turns toward her. "What are you going to do next?"

"That's what I wanted to tell you, Bran. I was offered a job in a restaurant in Beverly Hills. It's an elegant place."

"Is that what you want?"

"That's just a way of meeting someone with lots of money, so that I can live a good life. I might even try to become a model. That's another job they thought I could do."

"What's a model?"

"Someone who wears the latest clothes and has their picture taken for magazines."

Bran let that register although it seemed a useless way to make money.

"I've got the body for it, they say."

"You're very beautiful, June. I mean it."

"Thanks; which brings me to another reason why I wanted to take this walk." She stops and turns toward him with a look of earnest affection. Her lips are pressed shut and he finds himself admiring the ripe, soft allure of them. June's narrow eyes wander over him, and she smiles as she reaches up and strokes his cheek quickly then draws her hand away as if she knows it isn't hers to caress.

"You want to turn around, before we get mugged?"

"No. Not till I've gotten it all out." June swallows and looks at his chest, looks back at his eyes and says, "I want you to know that I'm happy to be here, Bran, because the choice is mine, not Dr. Shiksal's or anybody else's. It's as I said before. I'm free; free to make mistakes or take advantage of opportunities but the yes and the no will be mine and mine only. And I want you to know that I'm grateful to you." She stops and takes a deep breath. "If you hadn't come along, I'd still be back there in my comfortable cocoon just dreaming of freedom."

Bran feels a flush of embarrassment. "All I did was put my shoulder to the gate."

He starts to turn back but she reaches up, catches his shoulder, and holds him as she looks at him, her eyes now intense, even tormented, as she says in a dusty, quivering voice, "And there's one thing more." She hesitates, bites her lip, and looks down. Her head seems to shake a little as she looks into his eyes again and says, "You're my first love, Bran. You've given me that too. I know nothing can come of it, but I wanted you to know." Her brow creases, tears film her eyes, she draws closer to him and presses her head against his chest.

Something melts inside him. For just an instant he feels out of place, until a wave of tenderness envelopes both of them and he clasps her to him. June looks up at him, her lips parted, a single tear runs down her cheek and Bran kisses her with affection that borders on love. They kiss again, a kiss of separation, and without another word, they stroll back, hand in hand, through the flaring music and the garish light.

THE ELEVENTH DAY

—1—

"Wake up!" Bran pulls himself out of a heavy sleep to see Nikanor, dressed and serious. "Get up or you'll miss the plane," Nikanor whispers.

"It's the middle of the night."

"Change of schedule. We leave in three minutes. No time to brush your teeth." Nikanor shakes Ephus, "We're goin' in a minute. Hop into your jeans."

Impatient to leave, Nikanor stands over them as they dress. Only five minutes before, a young priest had come to his room to tell him that the Militants are looking for him. A car is available, and the priest will drive him to the plane so that they can take off before the Militants catch up with him. Rudolfo must have gotten the message that he is pulling out of the raid. Hopefully all he wants is to talk. But that is improbable, what with the death threat. He can talk from a phone booth in Reno but surely not in person. Although Unity's two planes take off from any one of five locations, each one is known to the Militants. Fortunately, they can't possibly know that he is flying to Reno, let alone know from which landing strip. But they would surely come to the Hostel.

The priest comes up to him. "A single car has just pulled up. Only two men in it, but even so, we shouldn't take any chances. We must leave now." He gestures to Bran and follows the priest out the door without looking back.

Bran picks up his shoes and trots after him on the smooth cold floor once again wondering what dangerous complication Nikanor has led him into. Downstairs another priest is waiting with a brown robe. Nikanor grabs it and flings it over his head without stopping. Seeing this, Bran wonders if it is too late to back out and make his own way home. But the prospect of returning on the same day is irresistible. He shrugs off his doubt and follows Nikanor down halls and out a back door into an alley.

The priest proves to be a fast driver and the car speeds through largely deserted narrow streets toward the devastated San Fernando Valley. Nikanor keeps looking back at every sign of approaching headlights.

They are again in the San Fernando Valley, much closer to the epicenter of the quake, and the car is following a circuitous path to reach their destination because of the many fissures in the streets and to eliminate any possibility that they might be followed.

The little single engine airplane is parked in an unlit yard of broken asphalt that was once a school playground. It looks flimsy to Bran, both too heavy to get off the ground and too fragile to hold all of them. Bran is not at all surprised to see someone he takes to be the pilot doing something to the engine by the light of a single flashlight suspended by a wire over the cowling.

"I'm changing an oil pump gasket," he explains to Nikanor.

"How long will it take?" Nikanor asks, sounding earnest if not anxious.

The pilot pulls his head out from under the cowling and glares at Nikanor. He is a middle-aged man with sandy hair shot with grey and large eyes rimmed with dark, bruised looking skin. "You never can tell. I might find the pump's shot, and then you'd better find another plane if you want to get there today." With that, the man turns back to his operation and Nikanor shakes his head and looks in the general direction of the street. They eat fresh rolls brought along by the priest and stand in the morning chill watching the violet light suffuse the sky above the ragged mountains until the line above the ridge shows the first pale yellow of the advancing sun. Nikanor looks at his watch. "Can I help?"

"Sure, by staying out of my way."

"Hank could get a bathtub to fly," Nikanor quips, perhaps to ease Bran's anxiety. Hank pulls his grease smudged head out of the engine cowling, closes it and swipes at the grease on his forehead with an oily rag.

"Let's go," he says, and they climb into the cabin, Bran and Ephus in the back. He pushes a battery of switches, the engine whines and coughs faster and faster until it smooths out into a deafening buzz. He taxies into the empty street and turns. "Anything coming?" he shouts.

"Wait till this train passes," shouts Nikanor. Bran feels a lump rise in his throat and he grips the torn seat arms as the plane bumps, bounces, shakes, and finally seems to be floating. He looks at Ephus's gleeful face and hopes that he won't be sick.

The faded autumn landscape unfolds beneath them, rumpled as a worn shirt tossed in a corner. Edging the land, the Pacific Ocean reaches out to embrace the horizon. A bird sees the world this way, Bran thinks. He looks at the back of Nikanor's mottled wooly head and it comes to him that Nikanor sees the world from high up as well. His own view is as cramped as the Glade, wedged as it is, tight as a foot in a boot in its tree staked valley. Nikanor, it seems, has a vision of California, even all of America, as it once was, a quilt like the one stitched together from pieces of old cloth that Leah has made for his and Mavis's bed. Bran looks down at his hands, limp on his thighs, and thinks of people, as different as their fingerprints. Is Nikanor right? Does every person have some responsibility for a stranger? There are no rules to life except that every living thing tries to keep on living, itself and through its offspring. This is all, Bran thinks. Ephus knows that better than anyone. He looks at the boy already asleep, his head vibrating against the wall of the cabin. Just try to stay alive and get as much pleasure and comfort as you can. Do the best you can to handle problems and go on from defeat to the next event hoping to win. If you don't ask for the Moon you'll be happy with a little piece of the Earth, Leah always said. Nikanor goes further than that. He believes that the rule of life extends to strangers. Humans, like all living things, have to keep humanity going from generation to generation. Most people can't help falling into sex, most women can't stop wanting to be a mother and nurturing their young until they are strong enough to fend for themselves. It is the basic rule. If you stopped it, life stopped.

He looks out the window of the noisy plane doing what it shouldn't be doing, floating over the land, not looking like it is moving, yet speeding faster than anything on the ground. People have created this machine to fly as only birds have flown. Not so long-ago people had almost destroyed life by overtaxing the soil, poisoning the air, poisoning themselves. These same people who must have had children and loved them and wanted a future for them, had taken that future away. What happened to them? They weren't farmers or gardeners, Bran muses, or they would have known better. It wasn't pragmatic because it didn't work. Maybe they just didn't understand life. How many of them had ever crumbled soil in their hands and tried to imagine what makes things grow in it? They had lost touch with life. They had confused life with possessions. They had done things without thinking out the consequences. It is enough if it works. Maybe even pragmatism could be carried too far. Or maybe they never even thought about it much. They just lived their own lives and let things happen.

He looks down at the brown quilted earth and sees it, not as separate valleys and towns but as a whole. Then it strikes him. That is what Nikanor is trying to say. If you just live in your own narrow valley and don't bother about what is happening in the next valley, strangers might do something that harms you and your family. That's why he and his mother had been on the road, because people hadn't cared enough to find out what was happening and do something to stop it. They must have thought that it was enough to take care of themselves and a few others. He has spent the last ten days tied to strangers. Every one of them, at one time or another, has risked his own life for the other, and somehow they have all come through it.

"That's Templeton," the pilot shouts over the roar of the engine.

Bran looks down. It seems even smaller, less significant, in its barren dish of treeless land. But the contours of the ridges and distant mountains are familiar. Their outlines spell home and seeing them makes him feel relieved, satisfied, and eager to see the Glade. The plane circles, banks, and drops ever closer to the town until he can even make out the patterns of faded grey and green paint, even identify a few of the derelict pick-ups, and the old men sitting on the benches in the square. The engine whispers and they float, then jar to the ground and bounce along the ruts of the sloping, pitted field that serves as Templeton's airport.

Nikanor climbs out on the wing, jumps to the ground, and Bran and Ephus follow. Nikanor looks at Bran and smiles. "A lot faster than going, wasn't it?"

Bran feels a flurry of affection for the man who has both helped and hindered him; affection, respect, and regret at the prospect of never again seeing him. He has no idea what to expect at the Glade but he has the feeling that he could use Nikanor's help now as much as ever. He tries to think of something to say but all that comes out is, "I hope to see you again some time."

"Maybe I'll just drop in on you some day," The two men look at each other thoughtfully, then Nikanor bends down, runs his large hand over Ephus's shoulder and arm and says "You be sure that your friend stays safe, Ephus." He reaches into his pocket, takes something out and hands it to the boy. "While you're in town, Bran, you'd be wise to go over and register that land patent even before you go home." With a wave of his hand Nikanor gets back into the plane.

"Nikanor," Bran shouts. "Take care of yourself!"

"You too."

Ephus and Bran watch as the plane rolls away and turns. With the roar of a giant bee it races down the field and gains the air. They watch as it rises and with a wave of the wings the flying thing, no bigger than a hawk, recedes toward the high spine of the Sierra until it is no bigger than a fly. Bran takes Ephus's hand

and together they walk toward the town gate. The town guard shambles forward with a kindly look and mutters from under his drooping moustache, "Ain't seen you in a while, Bran."

"I've been away. You heard anything about the Glade?"

"Still there far as I know." The guard breaks off in a wheeze and a spell of coughing and Bran quickens his pace, impatient to get back home, but eager to register the patent.

Ephus tugs at the sleeve of his blue, work-shirt, "I'm goin on. I don't wanta go in there." Bran tries to convince him to stay but there is no moving the boy and he turns about and walks down the road. Bran walks through the gate and down the familiar pitted street. It is as if nothing has changed in the last ten days; the same faded red pick-up truck in the same place as if it has been planted there, the familiar worn old men in their worn old clothes sitting in the square. He passes the café, a woman selling bread laid out on a blanket, and ascends the sagging wooden steps of the Forest Service Administration Building. Bran wanders down the hall and sees the Land Registration Office. A thin clerk, with hair plastered across his scalp in shoestrings, puts aside the magazine he is reading, takes Bran's papers, and examines them without looking up. He pulls out a heavy book, covered in light grey cloth, opens a page, and writes an entry in it. He stamps the document, keeps a copy, and returns one to Bran, with the sole comment, "Fourteen dollars."

He pays the fee with a sense of anti-climax and leaves the room wondering if it makes any difference that a few words have been scrawled in a notebook by an indifferent clerk. On his way out the main door it comes to him that he should visit Captain Webb and tell him about the patent. He has seen the Captain once or twice from a distance but would not have presumed to take any problem to the man in charge of the whole District. Still, he has a reputation for fairness and is hard on law breakers.

Bran wonders what Nikanor would do as he approaches the door with " Captain Webb" painted in black on the frosted glass. The door opens and an old man, nearly as tall as Bran, comes out and almost collides with him. He has the appearance of a scarecrow. His once firm muscles have wasted away leaving behind an oversized, useless skeleton. Captain Webb gazes at Bran with his observant, watery grey eyes.

He is about to walk on when Bran says, "Captain, I wanted to tell you that we've got the patent to the Glade."

The Captain stops, and wiping his close cropped liver spotted head with his dry hand, he looks at Bran as though he were trying to recall just who he was. Bran hands him the document. The captain brings it very close to his eyes and returns it with an oblique smile. "About time."

"Will that keep the people out that want to open the mine?"

"That's between you and them," says the Captain in his flat, slightly cackling voice.

"You mean you won't do anything to keep them off of our land?" says Bran, feeling indignation rise into his neck and face.

"We don't put up with trespassers," says the Captain. "If they want the mine, they've got to deal with you folks. Now if you'll let me pass," and Bran watched him stiffly cross the corridor to the door marked "Men."

—2—

The town behind him, Bran climbs the ridge and drops over its edge, descending into the ravine—two steep cliffs broken with massive granite outcroppings between which tall white-bark pines cling to shallow crevasses. Where the two cliffs join, a shallow stream is split by great rocks, tangles of logs, and upturned roots brought down in winter floods. Like all Sierra streams this one has many moods. Tranquil as an old cat in the summer, it becomes a roiling flood in the spring when the melt of the snowpack is at its peak. Bran is glad to see it refreshed by recent rain but still benign. Expectant, Bran steadily climbs toward the summit of the west ridge at last reaching the sentinel fir from which can be seen the first broken view of the Glade. He peers through the branches and leans against the rough bark of the tree to catch his breath, relieved to see the Glade unchanged. Skidding and sliding, he crosses the switchbacks of the path that traverse the steep slope.

The sight that meets him, when he reaches the bottom, surprises and disturbs him. Three cabins closest to the road have been reduced to charred piles of wood. His jaw locks at the sight of the blackened remains as he thinks of the Farleys, an old couple, both in their eighties, and wonders if they had gotten out of the cabin uninjured. It could have happened in daylight; a high wind could have spread it from one to the other. He scans the Glade looking for other signs of destruction and is reassured to find it as before, but not quite the same. The valley seems smaller than he remembered it, the ridges steeper, at least as compared with the great Central Valley. Having seen the many-tiered buildings of the cities, the cabins, uniform rectangles of rough planking, silver-grey from exposure like the hair of those who built them, seems smaller and shabbier. There is a sense of neglect; the raised beds of the vegetable gardens, not yet stripped of the summer's produce. Across the way, a pane of glass in Jorgenson's window is cracked, and the wood logs are still not split, stacked in a great pile behind the kitchen as if no one would need them this winter. It chilled his spine to think that he has returned to a hand-full of defeated hangers on.

What he sees next is even more ominous. A yellow panel truck and two yellow bulldozers are parked between two cabins at the base of the opposite ridge just below the scar of the tailings from the old mine. And as he hesitates, wondering what to do, a man carrying a shotgun approaches him shouting, "This place is posted. Nobody's allowed in here without a permit from Standard." Bran simply waits silently until the guard comes up to him, thinking in the short time he has how best to deal with him. "I saw you come down outta the trees," the man says as he comes within an arm's length of Bran. He is a head shorter than Bran, but his chest and shoulders are broad, and he has the oaken, wrinkled face of someone who has spent his life outdoors. While not pointing at Bran he holds his gun in a way that suggests he will use it if he has to. Bran gazes at him calmly assuming that he could persuade the man to let him pass; this is after all his home. "The road's posted since yesterday and there's a guard out there that wouldn't have let you in," says the man speaking with a nasal whine that sounded foreign to Bran.

"I live here. I always come through the trees; it's the shortest way."

"Not no more you don't live here. You must a knowed that."

"I've been away. Where is everybody?"

"Some's made camp up stream. Some's cleanin' up to clear out. We're gonna knock most of these shacks down tomorrow with them dozers," he says, swinging the gun toward the machines.

Bran feels the blood rising in his neck but he holds his temper. He has the patent in his pocket but it wouldn't make any difference to this lump. He has to show it to the one in charge. "Let me talk to your boss."

"He's up the mine. But he won't talk anyhow. If you want to come in you got to see Pollard in Templeton. He's the big boss. Nobody takes a piss around here without askin' him."

Bran has no choice but to take the gun. Besides he might need it before he is done. "Thanks," he says and he sees the man's expression relax as he feints a turn. As if to prod him the gun swings toward him but the man's finger isn't near the trigger.

With a quick lunge of both hands, Bran seizes the barrel, swings it toward the sky, and forces the guard back, tripping him with a leg shifted behind him. As he falls, Bran kicks him under the kneecap and falls on top of him, slamming the horizontal shotgun across his neck like a bar. The man lunges up nearly rolling over, but Bran resists and gradually presses him down to the ground, again smashing the shotgun against his neck and putting all of his weight on it to choke the man into submission. Although his face is red and his eyes bugging, the guard tries again to force him off.

"Let go of the gun," Bran snarls, "or I'll smash your windpipe!" The man's mouth is open and he is gasping as Bran thrusts down against his neck. Twice he does this until the guard goes limp and he releases his grip on the gun. Bran gets up slowly, pointing the shotgun at the guard's head.

"Strip. Lie face forward on the ground, arms behind your back." The man complies. With the belt he tightly binds his wrists running one leg of the man's pants through the loop. He stuffs a piece of his shirt into his mouth and marches him to the nearest tree at the base of the ridge. He cuts the man's pants legs, twists them into a rope and binds the man's legs. Then he loops the cloth rope to the belt and leaves the man on his stomach, hands and feet tied together behind his back, as a sheep might be tied before shearing. "Sorry, but it beats knocking you out with the gun butt," Bran says as he walks toward the kitchen, drawn by the reassuring wisp of grey smoke from the chimney.

The rough kitchen door is open a crack. He pushes it silently and walks into its comforting warm twilight, welcomed by the familiar smell of vegetable soup. There, sitting with her solid round back to the door at the wide pine table is Leah, her grey-streaked head bent as she works, and he feels a rush of tenderness for her. "Is it too early for dinner?" he asks and she, looking wide-eyed and startled, then overjoyed, clambers up overturning her chair. She wraps him in a hug, and he returns her wet kiss. She lets go, sees him wince from a pain in his shoulder, and immediately asks if he has hurt himself.

"You can see for yourself; I'm fit as a market hog. What about Mavis?"

"With the children. She's fine."

Aware of a drop in her voice he asks with foreboding, "Anybody hurt when the cabins burned?"

"Peter's gone. Shot. He took one of them with him though." She breathes a deep sigh that catches as she holds back tears. Sorrow and sympathy pass through him as he recalls her headstrong, often belligerent, son who had never liked him.

Leah turns away, a choking laugh comes out of her. "He was true to himself to the end. He took on the fire starters with a varmint rifle all alone and stalled them long enough so people could get out of their cabins." She looks down at the floor.

"I've got the papers for the Glade, if it isn't too late."

Leah claps her hands and her heavy dewlaps sway. "Not a minute too soon. They act like they own the place already. Telling everybody when they have to get out to make room for the mining crew. Would you believe, the boss, a red faced bull named Slone, asked me if I would stay on, and cook for them. He says they've got jobs for five or six healthy men who can stay with their families." Leah looks at him with widened eyes. "You mean you really got the patent to the place, after all these years?"

"Got it right here next to my heart." She gawks and puts her fleshy hand over her mouth. "You better show it to Slone. He's up there now," she says looking up in the general direction of the mine. "That shotgun might mean more to him than that piece of paper though."

"First I want to see Mavis,"

"They'll stop here on the way down anyway. I'll tell them you've got something for them. Take some bread to give you strength. You must be hungry. Did that food I gave you last you very long?"

He waited while she cut a thick slice of course brown bread and slathered it with honey from their own hives. "Where'd you get that shotgun?"

"From the guard; I hog-tied him with his belt."

"Aren't you something."

He drops his pack in the corner and feels unburdened for the first time since he had left on his journey. Then, honey dripping onto his hand, the shotgun in the other, he runs toward the children's lodge eager to see Mavis.

Except for Leah, Mavis, and the younger children, the Glade is empty. Leah has confirmed that the others are at Coffey Meadow a mile up the valley, building some makeshift shelters where most of them could spend the winter. The Forest Service has let them do that since they had planned to put some summer cabins on the meadow for service workers. Feeling like a kettle about to boil, Bran follows the familiar path laid between gardens fenced with homely, linked stakes and the shallow stream. Mavis and the children must all be inside, he thinks, as he approaches the building at the far end of the Glade that serves as nursery and school. He looks in the window and sees Mavis passing out goat's milk in brown pottery cups and bread to the six youngest children. The sight of her soft hair, faded gold streaming down the back of her pale blue shirt as she bends down to hand the milk to a child, makes his heart dance. He watches as the bread falls from the child's hand to the floor and she hands him another square, Mavis turns toward him, and he sees a sad look in the narrow, forget-me-not blue of her eyes. She looks up, and he watches as her expression changes from introspection to curiosity, then she recognizes him and it blossoms. She bounds to the door, flings it open, and flies into his arms. They cling to each other as though there is nothing else in the world to hold on to and he dissolves with love and longing for her, breathing in the fresh grassy fragrance of her soft hair.

She looks up at him through tear-filled eyes and says, in a broken voice, "You're finally back."

They both look about them for the first time and laugh at the sight of a gaggle of little spectators. Mavis shoos them inside, and sends Berry, an eight year old, to the upper meadow with the news of Bran's return. They sit down on the crude bench against the wall of the building, savoring the short time together before the others return.

"I've got so many questions," she says.

"I'll answer one. I got the patent."

"The rest can keep."

They sit silently for a while, shoulders touching, hands clasped, looking down the valley. Again and again they look at each other and smile. After only a few minutes Bran gets up. "I'd better go up and see that guy, the boss."

"Slone."

"The sooner we get rid of them the better."

"You think they'll just accept the patent and leave?"

"We've got to start with that."

"Should I come with you?"

"You'd best stay with the children until somebody comes back from the meadow." Bran looks toward the kitchen and sees Ephus coming toward him. "Here's my help."

"He ran off the same day you left."

"He's been with me the whole time, Mave."

Seeing Bran and Mavis, Ephus walks faster, staring at them, a secret smile on his tapered face. He barely acknowledges Mavis's greeting, and although he doesn't speak, his eyes lock on Bran's with insistence.

"Here's the hero of the trip," Bran says. "Without him I'd probably be dead right now."

Ephus ignores the praise and says, in a sharp, insistent tone, "C'n we talk? Just me and you?"

"I've got to go up to the mine. We can talk as we go." He kisses Mavis and walks away with Ephus at his side. As they walk, Bran's eyes turn to the familiar pebbled surface of the stream. Tines of grass undulate to the quiet flow and the soft rocks glow in subdued orange and brown. It's good to be in your own place, he thinks. His mind turns over what he might say to Standard's boss. He recalls the guard and hopes that it will be easier. He hadn't even checked to see if the shotgun is loaded. He breaks it at the breach and sees the circles of two shells. That should be enough.

"I'm not gonna stay here, Bran," Ephus says. I'm goin' back up over the ridge to live."

"Don't you like it here with me?"

"I like you. But I don't like the place much. People don't take to me, and I don't take to them."

"Give it time. You can't live alone. You're better off with people. That's what we learned on the road, didn't we?"

"Maybe."

"We'll talk some more, but now I want you to come up with me, get some throwing rocks and stay out of sight. If you hear me say 'come on now' to the men I find up there, you just let loose with some of those rocks to get their attention."

"Sure."

Ephus at his side, Bran ascends the path that parallels the mine tailings. Aspens, their leaves yellow, cling to the spare soil. The waste from the abandoned mine is a great welted scar, for the mine goes deep inside the ridge; how far no one at the Glade knows. The tunnel is blocked by a cave-in 200 yards from the entrance. Some believe that twenty men are still buried beyond it. He climbs toward the mine, thinking of the countless times when he had played among the weathered wood and rusted metal of the abandoned equipment.

Just below the shelf of the mine entrance Ephus hides behind a tree. Bran climbs on to the sunny, rock-strewn bench and looks toward the dark opening. Shotgun ready, he walks obliquely toward the tunnel mouth, avoiding debris and rusted metal shapes overgrown with bushes and weeds, staying well out of the line of sight. Hollow, strangely magnified sounds of men's voices echo from the opening. Just at the entrance he flattens along the wall and rehearses in his head what he will say. He shouts, "Come on out of there. You've got no right to be here anymore."

A voice bounces out of the mouth in response, "Who in hell says we don't?"

"I'm from the Glade. I registered the patent today. You are poachers now." He clutches his gun, pointing it toward the entrance, calmly breathing the cool, dank breath of the mine. His finger touches the trigger, and he resolves to shoot if he has to.

"If you got a complaint, tell it to the boss in Templeton. We got work to do in here." It is the same voice, probably the boss, he assumes.

Even before the echo of the response has died, Bran shouts back, "If you don't come out before I count to five, and with your hands over your heads, I'm going to dynamite the entrance and you can spend your life in there, what's left of it." Bran smiles to himself as he says this. Nikanor would be proud of him. He hears an agitated whisper but can't make out the words. He begins to count. "One...Two..."

"OK. We're comin' out." A cone of light is the first to come out and the sound of boots clattering on the loose rock grows louder. It sounds like two men.

"If you come out of that hole with a gun I'll shoot without warning," Bran shouts.

"You got a gun too, huh. What else you got?" The voice is rough but calm.

"Just the paper that says you've got no right to be here."

A hand, palm up, showed in the tunnel mouth. "My name's Slone," the man says as he comes out, squinting around him. Bran turns to face him, the shotgun pointing at his stomach. In his middle fifties, Slone has the square torso of a man who has done heavy work all of his life. His head is large, seamed with small red veins that made it look inflamed or angry, but the small blue eyes look at Bran with little more than indifferent curiosity.

"If you come up here lookin' for a job you picked a helluva way to get my attention."

"I don't want a job. Like I said, I just want you and your men off this ridge. Where are the rest of them?"

"Cal. Come on out with your hands up. This guy out here's kinda nervous." A younger man with curly red hair and a freckled face comes out and looks around.

"That all?" says Bran glancing apprehensively at the tunnel.

"Just me and Cal. We're just surveying the place. If you don't believe me, go in and see for yourself." Slone cracked a tight grin. "Can I put my hands down?"

"Sure. You two start down the hill now and I'll be right behind you." The men turn and begin to walk, and he turns to follow them.

He has taken only a few steps when Ephus shouts, "Bran!", but it is too late, the bullet has already torn into his shoulder and thrown him to the ground. He recovers, still gripping the shotgun, to see Slone lunging toward him, arms forward, his hands already reaching for the gun.

"Now you'll get yours!" Slone cries as Bran rolls over, flares the barrel toward him, and pulls the trigger. Slone's eyes widen with surprise then shock as the shot peppers and shreds his left pant leg and he stumbles to the ground bellowing like a wounded bull. Bran skids and rolls to the shelter of the nearest bush and slips behind it, nauseous and lightheaded with the burning pain of his wound. He sits up and sees Slone clutching at his bloody knee, making no move after him. The red headed man is running and stumbling down the slope. Staring at Slone, Bran feels no pity for him, no remorse, only relief that he is still alive. The bastard deceived him. Even when they had no right be here they tried to kill him and his anger gave him strength and anesthetized his bleeding wound. "The second barrel's for you!" he manages to shout but his one arm is useless and he knows he couldn't aim the shotgun and pull the trigger with any accuracy.

"I got five more bullets for you."

The arm of his shirt is already soaked with his blood and he feels weak. It would be best to try to make it down the hill but he isn't sure he has the strength. Then he sees Ephus scramble toward him like a ferret.

"You hurt bad?"

"Just a bloody nick."

"Looks wors'n that to me."

"Come on out. I won't hurt you. Standard's not worth getting killed for is it?" Bran shouts.

"Who got that first barrel?"

"Your boss. But he was about to kill me."

"With what?"

Bran wondered how many more of Standard's men there were. By now the red head would be at the base. He could take the truck and go for the other one that is supposed to be on the road.

"You're bleedin' real bad, Bran."

"Seems like he's holed up in the tunnel for the winter. We'd better get down for some help." Bran whispers. "Here. You know how to work this shotgun?"

"Pull on this little hook?" Ephus says reaching for the trigger.

"Don't touch it now! It might go off." Bran hands him the gun. "Cover me. Keep your eye out for the man in the cave and we'll start down through the trees. If he comes out after us, drop behind something, wait till he gets as close as that tree over there and shoot at his middle."

Ephus answers with a grave nod. As soon as Bran gets to his feet he feels light-headed and begins to black out but he fights it off and continues, stumbling from tree to tree until he reaches the bottom of the slope. Ephus slides to a stop and crouches beside him, the shotgun swinging as he alternately looks back up the hill and toward the road.

"Careful with that weapon, Ephus. And get your finger out of that little hole!" Still in the shelter of the trees he sees Mavis running down the path with his rifle in her hand. From the direction of the kitchen, Leah is lumbering toward the slope with her favorite butcher knife.

Then he hears the engine and looks up, expecting to see another yellow Standard truck. Instead, it is a familiar green pick-up, moving slowly toward the kitchen, and for the first time in his life he is glad to see the Forest Service. He gets up and cautiously walks toward the kitchen, clutching his limp arm. Leah gets to him first.

"Here, lean on me, Bran."

Breathless, Mavis stops in front of him. "I heard the echo of the shot and knew you'd been hit."

"Let's get him inside and deal with that wound before he loses any more blood," says Leah. Supported by both women and followed by Ephus, they move slowly toward the kitchen.

A Forest Ranger who he recognizes, spare and as dark as Nikanor, is leaning on the door of his truck, writing something in a notebook and listening to a crackling voice on the two way radio. "Looks like there's been some more trouble out here," he says, and seeing the wound he adds, "Let me help."

Bran sits down at the wide table in the kitchen while the two women and the Ranger clean and bandage his shoulder. The bullet has torn through muscle but made a clean exit.

"What brings you out here?" he asks the Ranger. "We haven't been cutting too much of your wood, have we?"

"You the one that bumped into the Captain and showed him your patent? He figured you might have some trouble convincing Slone. So he sent me out here to tell them to leave until they make a deal with you folks about the mine."

"We don't want any deals with the likes of them," says Leah, wringing out one of the towels she has used to clean Bran's wound.

Bran touches Mavis's hair with his good hand and looks into her eyes. Her love reaches toward him and flows through him, restful and reassuring as sleep.

"I'll go around and talk to all of them. I'll be sure they leave peaceably before I go," the Ranger says as he walks toward the door.

"One of them is wounded up near the mine," says Bran. "One's inside with a rifle, the one that got me. One's hog tied near the road. There are two others."

"I'll find them. It's my job to keep the peace." The Ranger stops in the doorway and puts his wide- brimmed hat on his head. "You take care of that shoulder. Come into town and see a doctor at the Service infirmary. You don't want it to get infected."

Leah stares at him as though he has insulted her. "We take care of our own out here."

"Things are a little different now. You're not outlaws anymore."

Leah sighs and looks around at the kitchen. "I almost burned the cabbage soup with all this going on!" She waddles to the stove and reaches for the heavy iron kettle. "I'll put some water on for tea. Ephus, how about a nice piece of bread still warm from the oven, with lots of honey?"

Bran leans back, nurtured by the words that he'd heard a thousand times in his life. He is home. It always came down to those words-the eating, the chores, the homely, comforting monotony binding every day to the next. A head, then two or three pass the window, and his heart thumps as he realizes that in just a few moments he would have to speak to all of them about his journey. He could tell the story all right, but there is more to say. The ranger's words echoed in his head. "You're not outlaws anymore." He thought of the welcome sight of the Forest Service truck.

The door opens and Thule comes in, looking toward him, curious, welcoming. Others follow, happy, respectful, or wondering. He will tell them more than the story of his trip. He thinks of Nikanor and June and wonders where they are, what they are doing, and he hopes they are getting what they wanted. He has learned about strangers, people who came and went, who made a difference, and who would always fill a space in his being. That's what he has learned and what he will share. He has learned to depend on strangers. More than that, he has learned to love them.

January 22, 2013, November 13, 2022
Sheldon Greene

www.ingramcontent.com/pod-product-compliance
Lightning Source LLC
Chambersburg PA
CBHW020936310726
48980CB00007B/799/J

* 9 7 9 8 9 9 9 4 9 5 3 3 4 *